DEVIL RIDERS

By the same author

Glory Trail
Hellfire Town
Arrowhead Valley
Buffalo Crossing

DEVIL RIDERS

BRETT PASCO

A Black Horse Western

ROBERT HALE · LONDON

First published in Great Britain 1994

ISBN 0 7090 5356 8

Robert Hale Limited
Clerkenwell House
Clerkenwell Green
London EC1R 0HT

Photoset in North Wales by
Derek Doyle & Associates, Mold, Clwyd.
Printed and bound in Great Britain by
WBC Ltd, Bridgend, Mid-Glamorgan.

ONE

There never was much trouble in the small Arizona town of Papillon, sitting in the curve of a sluggish creek feeding into the San Pedro River. Sometimes those who lived there used to regret that the world had passed it by; that life in Papillon was about as exciting as listening to a week of Reverend Buckman's sermons. Then they'd pay a visit down to Tucson, or up-country to Phoenix and come home glowing with satisfaction about the peace and tranquillity, and plain safety of their dull little home-town.

It was prosperous in a subdued way. Most of the land to the north and west was occupied by medium to large ranches. The huge eastern cattle companies hadn't started buying up land hereabouts yet, and the stores and merchants made a good living from the ranchers and their families. You'd get a wild bunch of trail-hands riding in now and then, but they had to check their guns in with the sheriff, and so the occasional fight generally ended up with nothing worse than a few bloodied noses and a lot more sore heads the next morning.

So nobody was quite prepared for what happened on that quiet Monday morning in September. Beck Fisher, who edited and printed the *Papillon Sentinel* was just on his way out of the office to go over the street to Tessie's Coffee House. As well as good strong coffee, the redoubtable Irishwoman who ran the place served up a good line in even hotter gossip which occasionally found its way into the *Sentinel's* pages.

Fletcher Murray, from the Crooked S, had brought his wife into town to do some shopping. They'd brought their six year old grand-daughter with them. She'd insisted that she was to stay in the buggy parked outside the draper's store. Stroking and talking to the sleek, good-natured horses was much more her idea of fun than listening to grandma clucking over some silly roll of cloth, or going to watch grandpa do some dull old business in the Cattlemen's Loan and Savings Bank. That was where Murray was headed now, and he gave the newspaper editor a wave as he walked smartly on his way.

The Reverend Samuel Buckman was already mounting the steps to the bank, carrying a hefty canvas bag filled with the assortment of coins he'd cajoled out of his congregation at yesterday's service. Another year, maybe, and they'd be able to think about building a spanking new church in place of the small, dilapidated building that had served them for the last fifteen years. They'd surely need it; the trickle of settlers moving into this part of the south-west was getting faster every year, and soon it'd be a flood. Papillon might be small now, but another ten years, and it might all be very different.

Then the placid silence of the town was smashed to pieces by the sound of pounding hooves. They came raising a mighty cloud of dust as they wheeled round the dog-leg at the far end of Main

Street. Eight or nine riders; big men on big-boned powerful horses, and every face hidden under a kerchief pulled up to the bridge of the nose. And they were headed arrow-straight for the Cattlemen's Loan and Savings.

Tessie O'Hanlon stared in horror out of the window of her coffee house as the riders swept past. 'Sweet Jesus,' she yelled to her brace of customers. 'It's the Arizona Devils come to Papillon!'

As they ducked to the floor one of them muttered, 'And I saw the sheriff and his deputy riding out just twenty minutes back! Guess the town's on its own.'

As the raiders dragged their mounts to a halt outside the bank, they blasted a wild volley of warning shots into the morning air. Four of the men swung down, and crashed inside. The town minister went tottering sideways as one of the bandits collided with him. The canvas sack fell from his hand, and he scrabbled to reach it.

'You seen the last o' that, Reverend!' yelled a rasping voice, and a vicious kick caught him full in the face, knocking him out and breaking his nose, sending him slewing back against the wall.

The terrified bank teller raised shaking hands, 'Don't shoot, please. I got five children.'

Another of the bandits, clad almost entirely in black, and plainly the leader of the gang, slammed a gun in his ribs, and threw a sack over the counter. Pale blue eyes glittered coldly. 'Fill it up, you hear? Quick, else your missus'll have to find a new daddy for the next one!'

At the same time, the portly bank president emerged from his office. He'd never admit to being hard of hearing, and now his growing deafness cost him the rest of his life. One of the intruders standing by the outer door spotted him coming out. Two deafening shots rang out, so close together they might have been one, except the bank president had a hole in his head and another in his chest. Spouting blood, he toppled forwards, some last dying reaction making him grab at the teller who was feeding the hungry sack with dollar bills from the safe.

With a horrified yelp, the teller leapt back from the dying man. The sack slipped from his hands, and his boss slumped face forward onto it. The teller backed away, ashen-faced. His hands and his shirt-front were soaked with the scarlet evidence of the bank president's dreadful wounds, and he was muttering raggedly to himself.

The man with the winter-cold eyes stared at him. There were some more shots from outside. As their echoes died away, he bellowed, 'Fill that frigging sack, I said!'

The teller couldn't move. His muscles had gone into spasm, and the only thing about him that was moving was his lips. The bank robber blasted out another oath, and vaulted the counter. He pressed the muzzle of his over-sized Colt to the side of the bank clerk's neck and pulled the trigger with a lot less regret than he would have felt at finishing off an injured horse. Then he dragged the sack, slippery with blood, from under the body of the bank president and wildly stuffed what was left in the safe into it.

On the floor the Reverend Buckman was moaning, starting to come round. He tasted the sickly flavour of the blood draining down from his smashed nose, and opened his eyes to see a gun levelled straight at him. He started praying.

'Leave him!' yelled the leader of the gang, as he swung the sack back across the counter, and then followed it. None of this had taken more than a couple of minutes, and now they were heading outside to their horses.

Fletcher Murray from the Crooked S didn't see them coming out of the bank. He was close to dying now, lying on his back some twenty yards away, twitching uncontrollably, with his revolver still clamped in his hand. He'd managed to loose off just one wild shot towards the mounted men outside the bank before a casual blast from a Winchester had taken away most of the left side of his face.

Beck Fisher was grateful that he hadn't been forced to try any such mad heroics. He never wore a gun, and now, still alive, he was pressed back against a wall, desperately trying to memorise every detail, however small, about the evil men who had ridden into Papillon.

They were all mounted up. A few more shots blasted into the air, they hauled their horses' heads round, and began to head back the way they came. Fisher jammed himself even harder back against the wall, and saw that the leading horse, a big black, had a white blaze, almost star-shaped, on its forehead.

'Susan. No!' Fletcher Murray's widow let out a heart-rending screech of panic from where she stood on the boardwalk outside the draper's store. The rancher's grand-daughter must have watched it all from the buggy. Danger meant little to a child her age, and now she was running towards the man on the ground. All she knew, with a half-formed woman's instinct, was that her grandpa was in big trouble, and someone had to go help him.

If the riders saw the child in their path they gave no sign. Beck Fisher recalled later that not one man had wavered an inch. They'd just carried on, and for a moment the little figure had been lost to sight among the flailing hooves of the galloping horses.

Then the riders were gone, the dust settled like a pall, and Beck Fisher, the newspaper editor, walked slowly into a street beginning to surge with folk with disbelieving, numbed faces. He couldn't drag his eyes away from that pathetic little body lying as broken and unrecognisable as a butterfly crushed under a boot-heel.

Kind of appropriate, maybe, he told himself grimly, since the town of Papillon had got its name from the French word for butterfly.

'What did the President have to say, sir?'

The white-haired man behind the broad expanse of desk, stared gloomily over the top of his spectacles at the much younger man who had just come into the office. 'What in hell do you think he had to say? There's an election looming like thunder-clouds, and he's got this business down in Arizona nagging at him. He can read the papers like everyone else.'

The tall, elegant young man, who'd never been further west than his native Philadelphia, gave a dismissive shrug. 'I think he's over-estimating just how much anyone really cares what happens down in that territory.'

'Well you go tell him that!' his boss glowered. ' 'Cause he blasted well cares. These Arizona Devils may be no more than a flea-bite to you, but they're biting the chief's butt just now, and so we've got to do some hard scratching. They're merciless killers.'

He paused. 'He's real upset about that massacre down in Papillon a few weeks back. 'Specially about that child who got herself trampled as they rode out of town.'

'Of course I read about it.' The aide swept a hand through his over-long hair, 'But there's no more than a dozen of them.'

The elderly man grunted. 'And they're causing as much trouble as if there was a hundred of them. Decent people starting to move in all across the territory. Arizona was just fixing to look as if it'd calm down, start to grow up, you might say. Now along with these so-called devil riders, we've also gotten a sizeable bunch of Apaches who've cut out from the San Carlos reservation causing their own brand of mischief ...'

The younger man butted in. 'Well, why can't the Army Department deal with this gang, at the same time as flushing out those renegades?'

'Because law and order is what we do, mister!'

'So we send in a posse of federal marshals!' He eyed his boss speculatively. 'That should do it. One of those special agents you've got working for you must have brought you some information about where they're hiding out.'

Not that he had any real hope that the Old Man, as everyone knew him, would tell him much. He was a law to himself in this corner of the US Attorney-General's department. It was common knowledge that he had his own network of informers and agents spread over those parts of this huge country where a civilised respect for law and order was still somewhat shaky. In theory he reported to the Attorney-General. In practice, he generally went straight to the President. It was a dispiriting place for an ambitious young man to work. Always the frustrating sense that something interesting was going on behind closed doors.

The Old Man dragged out his pocket watch. 'You had some reason for strolling in here?'

The young man gritted his teeth at the dismissive question. 'Yes, sir. I came to remind you that there's a meeting at two this afternoon about budgeting allocations for the different sections.'

The man behind the desk made a tutting noise. 'I guess you could go in my place. I get a sore butt and a sore head sitting in on such sessions. You can come back and tell me what they decided.' He sniffed, 'Which'll be nothing at all, if it's the same as usual.'

His assistant nodded. 'I'll do my best to represent this section's interests,' he said pompously. 'Though there are one or two pieces of information I'll need ...'

'Not now!' snapped the Old Man. 'There'll be someone waiting in the outer office right now.'

'There was nobody there when I came through.'

'He'll be there now. Just take yourself off, and tell him to come in.' He leaned back in his chair. 'Don't worry, son. You won't be stuck with me, much longer. I intend to retire soon. Take myself out West, and sit watching the sun go down.'

The other man stared uncertainly. 'I hadn't heard you were planning on retiring.'

'Well, I am. While I still got a few years left to me, I'd sooner be riding a horse than this chair. Now you just go do whatever you have to, and send that feller who's waiting out there in to see me.'

'I'll do that, sir.' The young man smiled politely, though his eyes were saying something different, and he turned on his heel and went out of the office. A moment later the door opened again, and a quite different figure entered. Sam McWheel was burly, grizzled, with a face leathered by real wind and real weather, and a buckskin jacket which hadn't been bought in a fancy store.

He gave an amiably crooked grin. 'You're looking fit'n well.'

The Old Man chuckled. 'No need to be so damned polite, Sam. I know you hate my guts. I give you all the worst jobs a man could have, sending you to God-forsaken places where I shouldn't send a dog, and you get paid less in a year than I earn in a month. Isn't that so?'

Sam McWheel lowered himself into a chair. As his deft fingers shaped a smoke, he said, 'I'd sooner be where I am, than where you are. Though sometimes I think it'd be kinda nice to be ... official. Wearing a federal marshal's shield and all.'

'Like that town in Nevada, Sam? You'd have been filled with lead soon as you showed your face if they'd seen a badge pinned to your vest.'

'Guess that's so,' conceded Sam phlegmatically.

'Anyhow, we seem to be getting somewhere now, Sam. You've done a good job so far. Sooner we get it all tied up in fancy ribbons the happier the President'll be. He's pretty sore about it all.'

'Not near so sore as the folks are down in Arizona.' The frontiersman shrugged. 'Most of 'em, anyways. They're kinda numb about it all. These boys just ride in, create more havoc than a buffalo stampede, then ride into nowhere.' He paused grimly. 'They're putting the fear of God into that part of the south-west. And they've come outa it just about unscathed.'

'There's that sheriff down near the Mexican

border claims he got one of them in the back, isn't there?' recalled the Old Man.

Sam shook his head. 'Maybe he did, maybe he didn't. We want 'em all, and that's the truth.' He lit his smoke. 'These boys seem to kill for the sheer enjoyment of it. Ain't natural.'

'Which is why they've been given that name.'

'Arizona Devils? Fancy name for a bunch of scum-brained killers. Meaner'n a raiding party of Kiowa sometimes.'

The Old Man nodded. 'That feller who just went out thinks we should send in the army, or failing that a federal posse.'

Sam sat there wreathed by a bluish halo of smoke. 'Does he now? We won't get to them by sending in a whole regiment of bluebellies raising dust. We'd never catch 'em in a hundred years.'

'But hell's bucket, Sam, we got more than a rough notion where they're operating from!'

Leaning forward, Sam extended a stubby finger, and jabbed it on the polished desk. 'They're surrounded by the meanest terrain in the south-west. They'd be scattered afore we got within twenty miles of them. You know that. We need to get at these fellers when they're out in the open. Need to know when they're heading off to some other small unsuspecting town and then spread a close-meshed net for them.'

There was a note in his voice which encouraged the Old Man. Cautiously, he said, 'You went to see ...?'

'Sure, I went to see that feller you told me about.' Sam sniffed, 'I reckon I come up with a plan.'

'Knew you would. Good one?'

'Won't take an army, that's for sure,' came the response, as Sam studied the smouldering end of his cigarette. 'Just me, and one other person. That's all. To start with, anyways. Might take a while.'

'Spit it out, Sam!' snapped the Old Man, testily tapping his fingers on the desk.

Blowing out a stream of smoke, Sam rocked back in the chair. 'I wrote it all down here, best as I could.' He handed over a couple of sheets of paper filled with scrawling, ungainly script.

The Old Man laid the papers down. 'Fine, I'll read that in a minute. I don't doubt the merits of your plan, Sam, however crazy it might look to someone else. It takes a while, the Chief, and everyone else will have to live with that. But you said you wanted to involve someone else.'

'Sure. Needs two people. Hell, that ain't asking much! Why you frowning like that?'

The Old Man waved a calming hand. 'I like to know who's working for me, that's all.'

Sam considered the remark, and then nodded. He reached inside his old buckskin jacket. 'Maybe you'd care to see a picture.'

'I don't care what they look like, Sam!' he exclaimed, as he was passed a small, crumpled photograph. 'I just need to know a few details.' Then he took a close look at the picture, blinked twice, and stared in amazement. 'Sam, you can't be serious!'

'Never more serious,' grunted Sam. 'Guess you'll want me to fix up a meeting. Just so you can make sure ...'

The Old Man pushed himself to his feet, and glared, 'Sam. This is crazy! This is a lump-headed notion if ever I heard one!'

'You want to put a stop to these devil riders, mister,' Sam retorted, 'I figure this is your best, maybe your only, shot.'

TWO

It had been a long haul from the town of Benson, up the edge of a rising expanse of prime river valley pasture. The sun was sinking in the sky behind them as the old Concord swayed its trace-jingling way into the cluster of buildings making up the Turkey Springs Way Station. The driver dropped down wearily and peered in at his three passengers. 'Last stop afore Charity, folks. You want to take a bite of chow, you got yourselves thirty minutes. Food ain't so good here, but it's filling.'

The fat man sitting across from Henry Deacon opened his eyes sharply. For most of the bone-shaking trip across this eastern part of Arizona territory he'd been slumped in a gape-mouthed sleep, snoring and spluttering like a steam boiler. He patted his huge belly as if checking it was still there. Henry found himself reflecting that the watch-chain stretched across his vest would have kept a family in food and supplies for a year. 'I guess a touch of supper wouldn't be unwelcome. You care to join me, son?'

'Can't say I feel so hungry,' said Henry.

Dragging out a red bandanna, the fat man dabbed the sweat away from his heavy jowled face and gave a wheezy laugh. 'You get yourself some food, boy. You need plumping up, if you're going to survive out here. I seen jack-rabbits with more meat on them. How about you, ma'am?'

The young woman sitting by the window along from Henry, started nervously when she was addressed. She was wearing a prim print dress with a frayed lace collar; her dark hair was gathered under her bonnet, falling into a loose knot at the nape of her neck. She'd hardly spoken the whole of the journey; sitting there with a tense, troubled expression on her pretty face. 'I don't think so, sir.'

The fat man grunted, and heaved himself along the worn leather to the door, and shoved it open. Puffing with the effort he got himself out, and then stared in at Henry, suddenly narrow-eyed, as if seeing him for the first time. 'Do I know you, boy?'

'Doesn't seem likely. First time I've ever been out this way.'

'Yeah, well, I guess that's plain enough. Maybe you and the little lady here got something to learn about being sociable.' His piggy eyes fixed harder on Henry. 'And you look real fine in your store-bought suit, son, real handsome.' He waved a podgy finger, 'But I tell you this for nothing. Wearing a fancy gunbelt don't make you a man, not 'less you can use it. And you'll find plenty of fellers in Charity'll be itching to see if you can use it.'

Letting out another unpleasant wheezy chuckle, he waddled off towards the stage station. The girl looked at Henry. 'He's hardly the one to talk about being sociable,' she murmured. 'He hasn't spoken all day, either.'

The large figure had disappeared inside now.

'He's been sobering up all day, I reckon,' said Henry. 'You must've smelled the whisky fumes when he climbed aboard at the Wells Fargo depot.'

'I guess I did,' she agreed. 'Anyway, I think I would like to get out and stretch my legs.'

Henry hesitated, 'If you'd care to come in and take a bite with me, ma'am, I'd be glad of the company.'

She gave him a careful sideways glance, 'I thought you weren't hungry.'

'Well, I wasn't hungry for his company.'

For a moment she was uneasy, that pensive expression returning to her narrow face, and then she nodded. 'I guess I am hungry, at that. But I'll pay for my own meal.'

'Sure,' he said mildly enough, though the fierceness in those last words had surprised him.

'I'm Henry Deacon, by the way. From California.'

'You've had a long journey.'

'Long enough. You come far, ma'am?'

'Only from Phoenix. I stayed overnight in Benson. My name's Mathilda Farnell.'

They shook hands gravely, then she gathered a shawl round her, and he helped her down. They watched the sweat-lathered team being led off to the corral. The three men riding shotgun on this trip were haggling over which of them was going to be able to go in and get a bite.

Henry grinned, 'Why can't you all go in? Stage carrying something valuable?'

One of the men, solid as a brick-wall, fired a warning glance at him. 'Folk round here get kinda twitchy at questions like that, mister. Might start figuring you was one of them devil riders.'

'Me?' Henry laughed. 'I'm from California. Devil riders?'

Mathilda plucked at his jacket sleeve. 'Let's go in,' she said anxiously.

'Sure.' He walked with her towards the stage station. 'What did he mean, that feller?'

'Haven't you heard of the Arizona Devils?'

'Oh, that's what he meant. Sure, I've heard of them. I thought they mostly robbed banks.'

The girl shook her head. 'I don't know much about them. Have you got kinfolk in Charity, Mr Deacon?'

'That's an ill-fitting name for such a rough kind of place.' He glanced eastwards, where the sun was throwing its dying light on the rounded peaks of the distant Chiricahua mountains, rising over ten thousand feet in places. 'No, I've got no kinfolk there.' They walked on to the station. The welcome smell of frying steak floated out as he held the door open for her. 'I might be staying there. I might move on. You?'

'I'll be travelling on again tomorrow, I guess,' she said.

The fat man was sitting at the long counter. He glanced round at them. 'Changed your minds then?'

'No law against that, is there?' Henry fired back. There was something about this one he didn't like. He was overweight, a drunk, and he had a magnified sense of his own importance. Deliberately he led Mathilda to the far end of the counter.

The fat man scowled, but any complaint he might have made was forestalled by the arrival of a tall, thin, middle-aged woman coming out of the kitchen. She put the plate down in front of him.

'There y'are Judge Blackitt. Steak and eggs, done just how you like 'em.'

He picked up his fork, and waved it at her. 'They better be!' he said sourly.

A faint frown crossed the woman's face, but she came straight along to where Henry and Mathilda were sitting, and the frown turned into a welcoming enough smile. 'What'll you folks have, then?'

Henry pulled his gaze away from the eating man. 'Steak and eggs, I guess, like he's having.'

'I'll just have a couple of eggs,' said the girl. 'And some coffee.'

The woman nodded. 'Coming right up. I know you folks ain't got time to sit around. Don't want the stage going off without you, do you?'

As she disappeared back into the kitchen, Henry drummed his fingers on the counter, and stole another look at the man called Judge Blackitt. In a low voice, Mathilda asked, 'Is something wrong?'

'Nothing that needs seeing to now.' He stared morosely through to the kitchen, where the cook was attending to her skillet. Maybe it was as well that he hadn't known he'd been sitting across from Judge Luther Blackitt just about the whole of the day. All the way from San Francisco he'd been storing up words to throw in that man's face. That'd keep for now, though.

He looked at Mathilda again, and slapped a cheerful smile on his face. 'From Phoenix, hey? I hear that's a growing town.'

'I didn't live there long,' she replied slowly. 'Came down from Kansas a few months back. My father died ...' A little shiver of sorrow went through her. 'I've been staying with my uncle and his wife.'

'I'm sorry to hear about your father,' said Henry.

'He'd been ill a long time.' Mathilda sighed. 'I had nowhere else to go. Things aren't easy for a single woman.'

'So why're you moving on again?'

The darkness in her eyes seemed to deepen, and her expression was as sombre as an undertaker's. 'I'm getting married. I'm going to a place called Diamond Rock to get myself married to a man I've never met!' There was a quaver in her voice, and her eyes filled with tears.

'A man you've never met? How come?'

Even as he asked the question, he thought of the answer. It wasn't unknown for women to travel west to marry men they'd never laid eyes on. Up in the mountains, in mining country, there were precious few women around. If a man had a mind to marry, there were ways and means of getting a wife. Henry had seen plenty of advertisements in the San Francisco papers placed by lonely men seeking company. But the women who replied weren't generally as young and pretty as Mathilda Farnell. They'd be older, widowed, maybe; or middle-aged spinsters trying for a different kind of life.

Mathilda was still staring at him; tears brimming over in her eyes, and Henry began to reach out an instinctive hand towards her. She pushed him away, though, and slid off the high stool. 'I'm sorry. I really don't think I could eat anything right now.'

She headed in swift panic towards the door, and Judge Blackitt paused thoughtfully in mid-mouthful to watch her go. But as Mathilda reached the door, her way was blocked by two new arrivals, burly cowhands in dust-caked range gear.

'Please, let me pass ...'

Obediently the men moved aside, and let her out of the door. Blackitt caught Henry's eye. 'Seems you got a real knack with the ladies, mister.'

'I don't figure that's any of your business!'

Blackitt slammed his fork down noisily. 'Now just what's gotten into you, boy? Blisters on your butt, or something, is it?'

The two cowboys came up to the counter, moving between them. 'You got two hungry men waiting out here, Sal!'

The woman came out of the kitchen carrying two plates. She stared when she saw Henry sitting by himself. 'Where's your lady friend gone, mister?'

'Seems she wasn't so hungry after all,' he said. 'Just leave the plate there. Maybe she'll come back presently.'

Sal gave an indifferent toss of her head. 'Long as it's paid for, don't make no matter to me.' She turned to the new customers. 'And how come you two need feeding in here? Ain't you got no bunkhouse to go home to, Archie?'

The taller of the hands shook his head. 'Ted and me ain't going back to the ranch tonight, Sal. Spotted Apache signs on the south boundary line. Mr Rand he wants a whole bunch of us keeping an eye out tonight.'

The other man butted in. 'Last time those red varmints rode down from the Cheery-cows they cut out fifty head.' He started building a smoke. 'And nobody saw nothing. Doubtless they was down over the Mexican border quicker'n that, selling 'em to some crooked *ranchero* for a few silver dollars.'

Archie nodded gloomily. 'And it's a whole waste of energy trying to watch for 'em. Easier to catch a shadow with a fishing pole. Still, Joe Rand's the boss. Anyhow, Sal, you go fix a couple of steaks for us. Can't stay around too long.'

She went back to her kitchen, and swallowing a mouthful of undercooked steak, Henry asked, 'You get much trouble from the Apaches?'

Both cowhands glanced at Henry. Ted laughed, showing a line of broken, crooked teeth. 'You don't need to worry, mister. They're just interested in rustling beeves right now. Your hair's safe enough, I'd say.'

Judge Blackitt growled, 'Nobody's hair'll be safe if they keep on getting Mexican silver to buy guns. It's about time those blue-bellies up at Fort Bowie started earning their money, and got those bastards back on the reservation where they belong.'

'And maybe they could take a look for the Devils while they're at it,' mused Ted. 'Course, maybe it's like some folk say, and those boys ain't flesh'n blood at all. Maybe they do just ride out of the dust, and then ride back into it.'

Archie grunted. 'Well, their bullets is real enough. And if they ain't human why're they so bothered about stealing dollars? They're men, Ted, jus' like the rest of us. Don't know which I'd choose 'twixt them and those Apaches.'

While they'd been talking Mathilda Farnell had come back in. As she reached the counter Archie shifted to one side, to let her sit down. 'I'm sorry, Mr Deacon. I had no call to do that ...' She eyed the plate of cold and congealing eggs, and reluctantly picked up a fork.

Henry grinned, 'Don't look too tempting, do they? But they won't do you any harm. And who's this feller called Mr Deacon? The name's Henry.'

From the other end of the counter, Judge Blackitt burst out. 'Deacon? Is that what they call you, boy?'

'My friends call me Henry.' He glared towards that unhealthily flabby face. 'So I guess you can call me Mr Deacon, Judge.'

The fat man got off his stool, and wiped a hand over his greasy mouth. 'I got the feeling I oughta know you. He was kin to you, was he? Lewis Deacon.'

'He was my brother.'

'The hell he was!' Now Blackitt strode down towards him, and stood close to him. 'You gotta nerve coming to these parts, mister!'

Turning right round on his stool, Henry faced him. 'How do you make that out, judge?'

Blackitt sneered. 'Bad blood runs in families, they say. Your brother was a no-good killer, Deacon! Only reason we didn't hang him was 'cause he died on us first.'

'What's all the commotion?' protested Sal, as she came out carrying the food for the cowhands.

Blackitt brandished a furious podgy fist. 'You know who this is, Sal? He's the brother of the murdering bastard who gunned down Stretch Finnegan.'

'Will you just stop crowding me, Mr Blackitt?' growled Archie, turning on the man standing behind him. 'Ain't too easy to eat with someone's elbow pushing your back.'

The judge stepped away a yard or two, but those small eyes still glittered in Henry's direction. 'Can't figure why you come here, Deacon. But one thing's for sure. You won't get much of a welcome in Charity. Stretch was a popular feller.'

Henry saw the two cowhands exchange a wry grin as they dived into their supper. He came off his stool sharply, and Blackitt, a head shorter than him, recoiled, backing off a dozen feet. 'Lew got a fair trial, did he? With you sitting there as the judge?'

'What you suggesting?' flared Blackitt uneasily. 'He got a judge'n jury like everyone's entitled to. Had himself a defence lawyer, too.'

'Spoke up for himself, did he?' snarled Henry, realising his fists were painfully knotted. 'Stood up in the courtroom and gave an account of himself?'

Blackitt wiped his hand over his mouth again, then dragged his bandanna out of his pocket and blotted his sweaty forehead. 'He was found guilty, mister. Stretch Finnegan stepped on the wrong side of your murdering brother, and got two slugs in the back for his trouble. We had five, six witnesses to that.'

Henry edged closer. The others at the counter had lost interest in their food, and were watching the confrontation. 'Before he ever got into that courtroom, Blackitt, my brother was beaten half to a pulp. He had a broken jaw, three splintered ribs, and both eyes so closed up he wouldn't have seen your ugly face from six inches away.'

Blackitt started to back away further, but now Henry wrenched at his wrist. 'You let go of me, you hear! I never touched him. Never saw him till they brung him into the courtroom.'

Henry kept a vice-like grip on the other man's wrist. 'No, you wouldn't have the sand to do it. And these hands of yours are too flabby to punch a hole in a paper sack. Lew wasn't fit to stand trial. The sense had been pummelled out of him.'

At last Blackitt managed to snatch his hand free. 'He got himself knocked about when he got captured. Lucky he didn't get himself lynched.'

'Oh sure, he was real lucky,' snapped Henry bitterly. 'Lew was an innocent man, Blackitt. Framed for a murder he never did.'

'Well folk round here don't see it like that,' retorted Blackitt. 'There was some wanted to string him up just the same, even though he was already dead.' He tried to look pious, 'I told 'em that wouldn't be right. Was me let his lawyer send his body back home to California. Don't you forget that. I know what's right, mister.'

'Well, I'm glad to hear it,' said Henry contemptuously. He'd never forget that first sight he'd had of Lew's battered face; hardly recognisable as the older brother he'd looked up to. His father had never recovered from the experience.

Blackitt tugged at his frock coat, trying to get back his dignity in the face of his interested audience. 'If you've come out here with some fancy ideas about proving his innocence, Deacon, you'd better think again. You'd do well to stay here tonight, and wait for the stage back tomorrow. 'Cause you ain't going to be welcome in Charity.'

'Is that a threat?'

'You take it how you like!'

'Anybody want coffee?' Sal's voice released some of the tension. Henry shot a final look of biting scorn at Blackitt and came back to sit by Mathilda to drink his coffee.

Archie glanced at him amiably enough. 'Maybe the Judge is right, mister. Nothing you can do now. Stretch Finnegan was one of the meanest buzzards in Charity, and had a whole lotta mean friends.

Ain't worth stirring up that hornets' nest.'

'I just want to get at the truth.'

Softly Mathilda said. 'It's none of my business, Henry, but it doesn't sound like the most sensible idea a man ever had. You said yourself, Charity's a rough place. I mean, I'm really sorry about your brother, but ...'

Henry finished his coffee. 'I always looked up to Lewis, Mathilda. My big brother. Sure, he was a wanderer. We had this shipping business back in 'Frisco. Started by my grandpa. Lew could never settle to working in the office.' He smiled nostalgically, 'Said there wasn't enough sky for him. So ... he just took off out here. My father always reckoned he'd come back one day, when the itch to wander had been well and truly scratched.'

She nodded understandingly, 'And he came back in a casket. That must have been hard for you all.'

Henry glared down past the cowhands towards Blackitt. 'Sure was. He was a lot of things, Lew, but he was no killer. And I intend to see that his name gets cleared.'

The stage driver poked his head in through the door. 'You got five minutes to eat up, folks, and then we're on our way. Charity next stop!'

The rest of the journey passed in silence. It was dark now, anyway, and Henry couldn't see Judge Blackitt's face, though he could sense his brooding, sullen presence. He itched to ask Mathilda more about what she'd said back at the stage station about getting married, but with Blackitt listening, he didn't want to ask.

The stage took half an hour jolting up a final steep grade, and then they came into the noisy, crowded streets of Charity, bright as day in the hissing, flaring yellow light of a thousand gas-lamps. More than once, as the stage made its final journey to the depot, Mathilda was spotted, and a face appeared at the window, as a drunken reveller hung on, and tried to make overtures at her.

She sat flushed, and embarrassed, staring ahead of her, while Henry yelled at them to quit bothering her, and Judge Blackitt leaned back, smoking a thin Mexican cigar and grinning all over his oversized face.

They pulled into the depot yard and things got quieter. Blackitt eyed them both. 'This town ain't for either of you. The Sagebrush Sodom they call it, when they're being real polite!'

'I'm not staying here,' muttered Mathilda. 'I'm going on to Diamond Rock tomorrow.'

Blackitt flicked the stub of his cigar out through the window. 'That so? And you figure things'll be more ... respectable there?' He laughed coarsely, 'Hell, compared to Diamond Rock, Charity on a Saturday night is like a missionary meeting.'

He shoved open the door. 'You got hard times coming, miss.' His eyes lit on Henry, 'And 'less you take care, mister, you got even harder times waiting for you.'

Lowering his bulk out, he picked up his valise which was lying on the ground. 'I'll get myself home, I figure. I won't wish you folks well, though. Ain't worth the waste of breath.'

He trudged off out of the yard, and Henry helped Mathilda down again. There was the distant sound of guns being fired; and the whoop of rowdy voices. She reached for a shabby carpet-bag, but Henry got there first, and hoisted it up, before picking up his own luggage.

'Where you figuring on staying, Mathilda?'

'I thought there might be a hotel near the depot.' She looked nervously towards the gates and the brightness of the town outside. 'Somewhere cheap. I couldn't see anywhere as we came through the town, though.'

'Let's go in the depot office. Maybe they'll know somewhere.'

The clerk, an alert looking youth with a stub of pencil behind his ear watched them come in. 'What can I do for you folks?' he inquired amiably.

'Well, I guess we both need somewhere to stay. Miss Farnell here's heading out tomorrow. Me, I'll be staying a while longer than that.'

'No trouble there.' The young clerk grinned. 'Just go out the gates and round back of the depot. My ma runs a boarding house. You'll see the sign nailed on the gate. It's real respectable, she don't allow no liquor in the house, and she's a real fine cook.' As an afterthought he added, 'She don't charge too much, neither.'

'That sounds fine.' Mathilda gave a grateful nod. 'That really does. I guess you can tell me what time the stage for Diamond Rock leaves in the morning.'

'Diamond Rock?' The youth took the pencil from behind his ear, and scratched his head with it. 'The line don't run out there no more, ma'am.'

She stared in alarmed disbelief. 'But I bought myself a ticket in Phoenix. Look, I'll show you …'

Before she could start hunting for it, the boy said apologetically, 'I ain't saying you're wrong about that, ma'am. Maybe nobody's told 'em up in Phoenix yet. Only quit running out there last week. Depot manager figured it wasn't worth it. Never had no passengers, and we was always breaking axles on that last grade.'

'Well how am I going to get out there?'

'Well, you could walk it, I guess. Though it's more'n thirty miles, into mountain country.' Then he grinned. 'But don't you worry none. Supply wagon'll be down tomorrow. Mr Gliss'll likely give you a ride back. Long as you don't mind his cussing and spitting, you'll be fine with him. Mind, my ma reckons he's kinda old to be driving a wagon ...'

'Is this Hiram Gliss you're talking about?' There was a tremor in her voice. 'He runs the trading post in Diamond Rock?' The youngster nodded, and she said, 'How old is he?'

'Mr Gliss? Heck, I don't know. Seventy maybe. Though he's that wizened-up, like a dried out old apple, could be older than that.'

Mathilda swung fearful eyes onto Henry. She was trembling, and now there was revulsion in her voice. 'That's the man I've come out here to marry! My uncle told me he was a good-looking man, no more than fifty-five years old.'

The youth eyed her uncomfortably. 'Heck, ma'am, f'r all I know Mr Gliss he's got a real nice nature, when you get to know him.'

Henry took Mathilda's arm. 'I'll take Miss Farnell round to your mother's place. You closing up soon?'

'Sure, any minute now, mister.'

Henry dropped a dollar on the counter. 'Maybe you'd bring our bags round, then.' The boy pocketed the coin with a grin, and Henry led Mathilda outside.

Whirling on him, she hurled her arms round him, and clung tight to him. 'Seventy years old? Henry, I can't marry a man that old.' She forced out a desperate sob, 'But what choice do I have?'

THREE

The sky was clear and the sun was up as Henry came out of Mrs Peacock's front door the next morning. It wasn't so warm though; the wind slicing off the mountains to the north east had a wintry spike to it. The Fargo clerk's mother followed him out, as he stood looking up the hill with its row of white painted frame buildings, each with a neat picket fence round it. This was the respectable end of town and no mistake. 'You say Judge Blackitt's place is up there somewhere?'

Mrs Peacock nodded. 'Sure is, Mr Deacon. Up there, top of the hill, just 'yond that big oak.'

'Guess he must make a lot of money out of his judging,' Henry stared up at the two-storied structure; imposing maybe, but probably as puffed up and self-important as the fat man himself.

The woman who ran the boarding house was a small, no-nonsense kind of lady. Folding her arms, she said disapprovingly, 'Certainly makes a lot of money out of something. Court fines f'r instance. Folk reckon the only real job Sheriff Ronson's got is to round up a dozen drunks most evenings so Blackitt can fine them the next day, and pocket the proceeds.'

'Is that so?'

Mrs Peacock shrugged. 'That's how it is out here. Blackitt owns a ranch too, over to the east, 'twixt here and the mountains. A silver mine or two, maybe. And he's got some property in Benson, I believe.'

Henry nodded. 'Doubtless why he was over there yesterday then. Collecting his rents or somesuch.'

'Or evicting his tenants!' snapped the woman. 'As long as this territory runs wild, it'll suit him.' Rather wistfully, she went on, 'Just hope I live long enough to see a touch of law'n order brought to Charity. Us folk at this end of town like to keep ourselves respectable but it sure is hard to keep going sometimes.'

Her gaze went up to the judge's house again. 'Just you take care, Mr Deacon. You tread on the judge's toes too hard and it might not only be him yelping!'

'I'l be careful, Mrs Peacock,' he promised. 'My father's lost one son, he sure doesn't want to be burying me as well.'

Last night he'd sketched out the bones of why he'd come here. It was her son Vinny who'd recalled that most people were glad to see the back of Stretch Finnegan.

'Least a hundred folk in Charity who might of shot him, Mr Deacon. Judge Blackitt might of been sorrier'n some, mind. Stretch used to do jobs for him, they say.'

'What kind of jobs?' Henry had asked.

The youngster just shrugged. 'I dunno, 'xactly. They say that when folks were late paying their rent, that Stretch might visit them.'

Now Mrs Peacock was eyeing him thoughtfully. 'I daresay you'll be going to see Grover Whiting, the feller that tried defending your brother at that so-called trial.'

'First on my list,' he replied. 'Right now he's the only one on my list.'

'Well, don't blame him too much for failing,' said Mrs Peacock. 'I doubt any lawyer could have won that case. Might be a lot of people to blame for what happened to your brother, Mr Deacon, but Grover Whiting wasn't one of them. A decent man, he is. And they're rarer than roses round here.'

'Heck, I'm not going to bawl him out about anything, Mrs Peacock, I promise you. He made all the arrangements to get Lew sent back to 'Frisco with Lew's body. He wrote us a real nice letter, too. But there's still a lot of questions I need to ask him.'

She nodded, satisfied, 'You'll find his office three doors down from the Paradise Saloon.'

'Thank you kindly.' He started to move off.

'Now I guess I'd better go wake Miss Farnell. Poor child was sleeping like a baby when I looked in on her.'

'Well, sleep catches up on us all, 'ventually.' Her face hardened, 'But it's not right, a pretty young thing like that getting herself harnessed to an old buzzard like Hiram Gliss. Deaf as a tree, and with a wicked mouth on him. And nearer eighty than seventy, I'd reckon.'

He blinked, 'You didn't tell her that last night, ma'am. That was kind of you.'

'She's gotta find out sometime,' she commented, and went on darkly. 'And from what I hear of Diamond Rock, it's even less of a place for a lady than this town. And that's saying something!'

'Well,' he returned, 'It's going to be mighty tricky to stop her going back with him. She's not the kind who breaks a promise.'

From what Mathilda had told them, it was moonlight clear that her uncle was using her for his own ends. He and this Hiram Gliss had been partners once, it seemed, and there was some old debt outstanding. Doubtless Mathilda's uncle had seen his way out of supporting his orphaned niece by offering her as settlement of his debt to the old man. A real suitable arrangement for all concerned; except the woman in question.

'It's indecent,' Mrs Peacock burst out, 'Like selling someone into slavery. I mean, you heard me tell her I could find her a job of some sort. Helping me out. Couldn't pay much ...'

'I heard you, ma'am. Trouble is she's too honest for her own good. But some deals are just meant to be broken, and that foxy uncle of hers needs teaching a lesson.'

The woman gave a sharp nod. 'He sure does! He wasn't a full sack honest with her. Telling her how Gliss was so charming and respectable.' She glowered, 'I'd sooner share a bed with a skunk.'

'Well, you just keep on trying to coax her into staying, ma'am,' said Henry.

'If need be I'll tie her down!' Mrs Peacock was distracted by the sound of footsteps hurrying along the hallway, and she swivelled to give her critical attention to her son. 'Now look at you, Vinny. You ain't brushed your hair, and that's yes'day's shirt you're wearing! You get back in and change it!'

'But ma, I ain't got time! Told the manager I'd open up the depot this morning. I'm late already!'

She chased him back inside. 'Never mind late! You go get yourself a clean shirt and comb that hair ...'

Henry grinned, remembering the way his own mother had hollered at him like that, and set off down the hill. If anybody could convince Mathilda Farnell to renege on her uncle's bargain with Hiram Gliss, Mrs Peacock could. He had problems of his own to worry about right now, though. Skirting round the closed-up Wells Fargo depot, he arrived at the head of the long, straggling main street.

The town was bigger than he'd expected. Main Street was mostly taken up with saloons and stores, with a couple of cheap rooming houses leavening the mix. But Charity sprawled sideways, too, with a jumble of shanties and larger buildings elbowing untidily away from Main Street.

There weren't too many folk around this Sunday morning; the stores were all closed up, and Mrs Peacock had told him that the nearest church was over in Benson. He came across a few men huddled in doorways, still sleeping where their drunken fancy had taken them last night. One of them, a grizzled old feller, woke up as Henry passed, and shot out a bony hand round his ankle.

Henry dragged his leg free, staring down. 'What's your game, mister?'

A pair of bleary eyes looked up at him. 'Can you tell me what day it is?'

'It's Sunday.'

The old timer grinned toothlessly, 'Well, that's fine, then. No need to wake up yet!' And he closed his eyes, and slumped back again.

Wondering just what they put in the local sourmash, Henry walked a few more paces along the boardwalk, and then realised he'd reached the Paradise Saloon. It was a legend even back in

'Frisco, this place, with its acres of mirrored walls and its dozen glittering crystal chandeliers. He'd been told that the Paradise's house-girls in their hip short skirts were prettier, and friendlier than you'd find anywhere else in the west.

The saloon's frontage took up a sizeable slab of the street, and as he peered through the tall windows into the gloomy interior he could see it was bigger than a dozen barns, with a ceiling half-way to the sky. Over by the wide sweep of the bar counter he saw movement.

It was an old Mexican in a long apron, pushing a brush in a lackadaisical fashion. The old-timer spotted him peering in, and gave a shake of his grizzled head, maybe trying to tell him that they weren't opening up for anyone at this time of the morning. Henry turned away, starting to walk on to where he'd been told he'd find the lawyer's office.

And then he stopped abruptly, as someone called his name. 'Deacon! I want words with you!'

He'd figured he was going to have to face something like this. Perhaps he hadn't expected it to come quite so soon. Taking a deep breath, he turned, slipping his coat back away from his holster. There were two of them out there in the middle of main street, and they clearly weren't set on wishing him a good morning and bidding him welcome.

The older of the two was heading for forty maybe; a squat, bull-necked individual in a grubby sheepskin coat, out at the elbows, over an even grimier red shirt, and with a purple kerchief knotted round his neck. He had a sagging cartridge belt buckled across his middle, packing what Henry recognised as a pair of cannon-sized Walker Colts. He tipped his hat back from his squashed-up face, as his companion moved away from him.

Henry shifted to the edge of the boardwalk, and stood there easily enough, his hands hanging by his side, as he watched the approaching figure. The second man was younger; wearing black shirt and levis. He had a pale, wasted face, and straw coloured hair poked out from under his high-crowned headgear.

'You boys are up early,' said Henry conversationally, and stepped down from the boards.

'You trying to be funny?'

'Trying to be friendly, maybe,' said Henry.

The pale-faced man came a few strides closer. There was a twitching nervousness about his movements, and his hand hovered near his hip, where he was a wearing a pearl handled Navy Colt in a holster cut away so far that the cylinder was exposed. 'Don't need friends like you, mister. I'm Dan Finnegan. Stretch Finnegan was my pa. Your brother shot him in the back.'

'Judge Blackitt told you I was in town, I guess.' Henry forced himself to speak with a casual coolness which he certainly didn't feel inside. 'You taken over your pa's job with the judge?'

Finnegan ignored the question. 'That brother of yours was guilty as hell, Deacon. A dozen fellers saw him gun my pa down.'

'Many as that?' said Henry wryly. 'They just stood by and watched him do it? Maybe Charity fellers aren't so tough as they make out.'

'You stay round and you'll see just how tough we are,' snarled Finnegan. 'Your brother should of hung for what he done. You start yattering on about how he was innocent, and you'll get folk turning 'gainst you.'

'Hanging offence, is it?' asked Henry placidly, 'Trying to get at the truth. What law book did you read that in?'

Dan Finnegan suddenly looked uneasy, though he tried to keep up the menacing bluster. 'Jeez, you talk real fancy, mister. You ain't the kind we want here in this town.'

'Well, thank you kindly for telling me. Always good to have things spelled out.' Henry gave a swift nod, and touched the brim of his hat. 'I'll get on about my business, now, if you don't mind.'

The older man joined in now. 'The boy's right, mister. You don't want to go stirring up things best left be.'

'Who says I've come to stir things up?' returned Henry. 'I just want to know the truth. Maybe the folk in this town didn't manage to hang an innocent man, but they killed him just the same.'

'You got real trouble coming to you, mister!'

Henry pulled his gaze back to Dan Finnegan. 'Did you say something, Finnegan, or was that just an old buffalo breaking wind?'

'Nobody talks to me like that!'

The man with the purple kerchief let out an urgent bellow as Finnegan's hand snatched for his gun. 'Dan, don't be a fool!'

A single shot echoed over the sleeping town, as Henry Deacon's slug sent a shower of dirt kicking up just inches from Finnegan's left boot. He eased the hammer back again, and moved his .45 to aim straight at the man's chest. 'Like your pal says, just don't be a jackass. Next time the slug'll go somewhere a touch more damaging.'

Both men gaped at him in astonishment as he reholstered his Colt. Finnegan stood like a stone statue, his fingers kind of jammed where they had been about to close over the butt of his own weapon.

His crony moved wonderingly alongside him. 'By gravy, Deacon, how did you do that? I don't figure I ever seen a man draw so fast.'

Finnegan found his voice. Shakily, he declared, 'Had it in his hand all the time, Pete. That's how he done it.'

'You know that ain't so, boy. He beat you by a mile and some.' Pete spat out a dark jet of tobacco juice, and there was a resentful admiration in his puffy eyes as he stared at Henry. 'Well, you sure ain't just a city slicker, mister.' He slapped the younger man on the shoulder, 'Come on Dan, you said your piece.'

Finnegan half turned, but then he swung back again, and his eyes blazed. 'Message is still the same, mister. You ain't wanted round here. Next time your fancy gun-trickery mightn't work. You think about that.'

They strode off and a moment or two later disappeared down one of the side-alleys. Henry took off his hat and fanned his face. He'd taken one hell of a chance there. Riling Dan Finnegan could have been his last living action. But he'd been determined to get the message across that he wasn't going to be shouted out of Charity. His legs felt kind of rubbery, but he grinned suddenly, and patted his holster. Not bad for a man who'd spent most his adult life sitting at a desk working his way through thick sheaves of shipping manifests.

A throaty chuckle sounded from behind him, and he swung round, startled. 'You'll have every gunslick in the place itching to try you out now, Henry Deacon.'

He saw a thin, wiry figure standing in an open doorway. Early morning it might be, and the man was still in his shirt-sleeves, but he had a dapper, well-groomed look about him. He twitched a hand at his white goatee beard, as Henry mounted the boardwalk.

'Mr Whiting?'

'That's me.' The elderly lawyer nodded in admiration as they shook hands. 'You going for that gun of yours was no more'n a blur. Where in hell did you learn to do that?'

'Did you ever hear of a feller called Chet Stookey?'

Whiting frowned. 'Name doesn't mean a thing. Any reason it should?'

Henry shrugged, 'Twenty years ago his face was plastered on sheriffs' walls across the whole length of the frontier. He rode with the Beagle Boys.'

'Well, I heard of them,' said Whiting. 'Bank robbers. A real mean crew.'

'Maybe,' agreed Henry. 'Though in all the time they were operating they only killed one man. And Chet still reckons that was an accident. A lot different to the mob creating trouble in these parts, right now.'

'You can say that again, and some,' returned the lawyer. 'They must have gunned down more than twenty people in the last year. Most of them unarmed. Small, peaceful towns mostly. Arizona's future, you might say. And this gang's threatening all that.'

He stopped, 'Anyhow, come in and take some coffee.' Henry followed him inside. 'So this old bank robber's been teaching you how to handle a gun, is that it?'

'That's how it is,' Henry confirmed.

They went past a smart office and on into the lawyer's living quarters, which were a whole lot less smart. Mr Whiting plainly had a system of using up every pot, cup and glass he owned until he ran short and it was time to wash something.

'The Beagle mob got snared up in Nevada eventually,' Henry explained. 'After Chet had served his time he came to California to live with his sister. She was a friend of my mother's. My father found him a job. Used to keep an eye on our yard down on 'Frisco Bay. The stevedores kind of lost heart for thieving once old Chet started riding shotgun there! And I figured that he'd be the one to teach me how to shoot straight.'

The other man sorted out two clean mugs, and filled them with strong black coffee. 'Well, he did a good job.'

Henry lowered himself into a chair. 'I spent a lot of time with old Chet over the last few months since you sent Lew back to us, Mr Whiting.'

Whiting leaned against the wall, and flicked a finger at his trim beard. 'I guess I knew I'd see you sometime, Henry.'

Henry nodded. 'Too many questions needed answering, Mr Whiting. My father never recovered after we buried Lew. Just seemed to lose heart in everything. Well, he's gone now. And I've sold up the shipping business.'

'Left California for good?'

Henry shrugged, 'I'm making no decisions, just

yet. Figured it was time I made some kind of change, anyhow. First thing I had to do was find out exactly what happened to my brother.'

The old lawyer's face was sombre. 'Well, I don't know if there's any hope of finding out what really happened, Henry.'

'I'm going to give it a damn good shot,' Henry declared. 'Somebody knows why Lew rode into Charity that day. Somebody knows why he was beaten into corn-mash, and why he was framed for Stretch Finnegan's killing.' He looked hopefully at Whiting, 'You've not thought of anything else?'

Back home they'd often wondered just what would have happened if a young deputy sheriff with a conscience hadn't brought himself here to the lawyer's office late that night. He'd told Whiting about a prisoner who was lying in one of the cells, more dead than alive. The trial had been fixed for the following day, and it was plain that nobody was about to try fixing up any kind of defence for Lewis Deacon.

The elderly man drained his cup. 'I've tried, Henry, believe me. Thing is, I had nothing to go on. Your brother was half-dead when they finally let me into his cell. They'd done a good job on him. He couldn't talk, could hardly see or stand up. Only thing he managed to do was scratch out your address on a scrap of paper.'

He shook his head. 'I did my best at the trial. But Blackitt never let me ask the so-called witnesses any real questions. Most of 'em were drunk, anyhow. If I'd had the time I might have tried to see the Territorial Governor, but Lew died anyhow. Started coughing blood in the night.'

'Drowned in his own blood,' muttered Henry.

'No way for any man to die.'

Whiting refilled his cup. 'Well, at least you managed to give him a decent burial.'

'Sure.' Henry knew this was all pretty desperate. The last they'd heard from Lew, almost a year ago now, he'd been in Phoenix, about to head back into the mountains where he was trying his hand at silver-prospecting. For some reason he'd brought himself down into Charity. But they didn't know where he'd come from, where he'd been living. There'd been nothing in his pockets. His horse had disappeared. He was like a man who'd ridden out of nowhere.

He looked at Whiting again. 'Thing is, though, Judge Blackitt wasn't too happy to see me. And from what just happened out there, it's plain he's already started stirring things against me. They got something to hide, and they're twitchy that I might find out something.'

The lawyer set his cup down. 'Yeah. But I can't rightly see where you're going to start. You stood down Dan Finnegan well enough, but the fastest draw in the world's of no account if they come at you from behind.'

'You think I should quit now?'

Whiting grinned grimly. 'Don't matter what I think. Might as well try fighting off a grizzly bear with a wooden spoon as stop you, Henry Deacon.' He tugged at his beard again. 'There's just one thing you could try.'

'What's that?'

'The feller that came to me that night. I always reckoned he knew a touch more than he was telling.'

'The deputy, you mean?'

The lawyer nodded. 'That's him. Marty Wilson. Gave up his job soon after. Married a pretty little gal called Shirley-May and moved right outa town. They got themselves a place out on the trail between here and Diamond Rock. Heard he was trying his hand at horse-rearing. You could try talking to him. But I wouldn't stack up your hopes. He was brown-britch scared when he came here. Might still be that way.'

Henry got to his feet. 'Well, anything's worth snatching at, Mr Whiting. Now I'd better be going.'

'Stay have some breakfast.'

'Already had breakfast at Mrs Peacock's place.' The mention of Diamond Rock had reminded him about Mathilda Farnell's problem. 'But there's a lady staying there I need to go talk to.'

Whiting grinned. 'You're a fast mover, Henry.'

'It's nothing like that.' Quickly he told the lawyer about the situation. 'You reckon she's got any sort of legal need to marry this Gliss feller?'

The old lawyer chewed it round before replying. 'He's a rich man by all accounts. Runs the trading post, and a log-cabin cathouse. Got himself a share in more than one silver mine round there. And he's mighty old. Could be that Miss Farnell'd find herself a real wealthy widow before too long.'

'And maybe he'll live to be a hundred,' burst out Henry. 'That doesn't sound like a good deal to me.'

'Could be worse,' returned Whiting slowly. 'And Gliss is a rough old buzzard. If she goes back on her uncle's agreement, he won't be too happy.'

'Nothing you can do to help her? You're a lawyer.'

Whiting sighed. 'Henry, I was a good lawyer once. Took myself off to Washington DC when I qualified. Hell, I had ambition then. Smooth-talking attorneys always had their eyes on politics as well as the law-books.'

'So how come you're down here, Mr Whiting?'

'Maybe I wasn't smooth-talking enough. City suit, backwoods voice, you might say.' The lawyer laughed ruefully. 'Came kinda clear I wasn't going to stand on any mountain-tops up North. Came down here to ... try again. And I do my best to practise law. But what that amounts to mostly is handling land deals, making sure that papers have the right number of signatures, or crosses on them.'

'Yeah, but ...'

'But nothing, Henry,' Whiting cut in. 'I couldn't do much to help your brother, and I can't make any promises that I could help your lady friend. Gliss and Blackitt are close as fleas, too. And if they got together ...'

With those gloomy words ringing in his ears, Henry came back out onto Main Street. Things were wakening up a little now. Most of the drunks he'd seen earlier had shifted themselves now. The general store across the street had been unshuttered, and an eating house next to it was pumping out the smell of bacon and coffee. The big doors to the Paradise Saloon had been opened, and just inside the doorway, a trio of girls wrapped in a froth of lace had pulled up some chairs and were drinking coffee.

Henry glanced at them as he passed, and in unison they winked at him. The one in the middle, her brassy hair hanging loose, leaned forward. 'Not seen you round here, before, feller. He's real pretty, isn't he, gals?'

He flushed and hurried on as they giggled uproariously and sent a few ear-burning remarks after him. Crossing the street, he headed past the Wells Fargo depot, and saw the stage-coach team being harnessed ready for the morning trip back to Benson. Mrs Peacock's son was doing his best to look as though he was supervising operations. He gave Henry a brisk wave. 'Howdy again, Mr Deacon.'

With a nod Henry hurried on up the hill. He had all manner of practical things he had to consider. If he wanted to get out to Marty Wilson's homestead, he'd need some kind of transportation. He couldn't pretend he was much of a horse rider. There wasn't much call for that in his trade. Some kind of buggy would suit him better. Right now though, he was wondering just what he could say to Mathilda. He'd pondered lending her enough money to buy herself a ticket out of Charity, but since she had nowhere to go, he couldn't see that would help much.

And then his nerves twanged as he saw the wagon standing just down from Mrs Peacock's place, with a scrawny youngster keeping a close watch on the restless team.

'Is this Hiram Gliss's wagon?' he demanded, as he raced up to the boy.

'Sure is. He gave me a nickel to mind the horses.'

'Where is he?'

The boy shrugged. 'Went on up the hill to the Judge's house. Said he wouldn't be more'n a few minutes.'

'By himself?'

'No sir. He went over to Mis' Peacock's place and come out with a lady. Then he headed off up the hill, and Mis' Peacock went chasing after him.' He grinned ruefully, evidently wishing he could have run up there too, to see whatever fun might be happening. 'She was hollering fit to bust.'

'I'll bet she was!' Henry blasted out, and hurled himself off up the hill. There might be all sorts of reasons why Hiram Gliss might be taking Mathilda up to see his pal Judge Blackitt. But he could only think of one. Blackitt might be a villain, but he was an important man just the same. A judge had all kinds of duties. One of them was presiding over courtroom trials. Another one was conducting marriage ceremonies!

FOUR

'You let me through, you hear, Barney Bates!'

Mrs Peacock was struggling with a heavily-made man blocking the porchway of Judge Blackitt's house. She hurled herself against him, pounding her fists on his chest. He made no attempt to retaliate, but just stood there as unconcerned and good-humoured as if she was throwing goose-feathers. He gave a rolling laugh. 'I'm real sorry, but you ain't coming past, ma'am. I got my orders.'

Henry came out from the shadow of the old spreading oak, levelling his revolver with a rock-steady hand. 'Step back, Mrs Peacock. Don't want you getting hurt.'

She twisted round. 'Thank heavens you've arrived at last, Mr Deacon. She's in there, Mathilda. Getting married to Gliss. We're maybe too late already.'

'Let's hope we're not! Now, you move aside, mister.'

The big man showed no signs of budging. There was even an amiable twist to his grin. 'Something tells me you won't shoot an unarmed feller, mister. You want me to move, you come move me.'

'Shoot him!' yelled Mrs Peacock. 'Don't kill him, though. His ma'd never speak to me again.' She glared at Barney, 'Though if she knew how you were behaving she'd likely shoot you herself!'

'Just calm down,' Henry shouted back. 'I'm not shooting anyone!' He thrust his gun away and considered his chances. Old Chet Stookey hadn't given him too many lessons on this kind of fighting. His general advice had been, 'If he's smaller'n you, young Henry, you take him on. If he's bigger, well you only take him on if you got no other choice.'

Mrs Peacock ran back to him, turning her back on the house, and staring pleadingly. She wasn't a panicky woman, but her hands were flapping like sheets on a wash-line. 'You can't just stand there, Henry Deacon.'

He looked over her shoulder towards the man filling the porch. 'I'm going to be no good to you if he lays me out,' he muttered. 'We could try finding another way in.'

'He'll only come after us,' she said. 'Mind, it's probably too late now.'

Something snapped in him at that idea. 'Will you hush up about that!' he yelled, and she recoiled at the ferocity in his voice.

'Now you talk nicely to the lady, mister!' called the guard warningly, his cheerful mood vanishing like icicles in the sun. 'No need for bad manners. Just act like a gen'leman, you hear.'

Henry blinked in surprise. Mrs Peacock started to turn. 'If you were a gentleman, Barney you'd let me inside.'

'Just stay looking at me.' Henry spoke swiftly, in a low voice as he grabbed her arm. 'We just want him away from that door.'

He slid his gun from the holster again, and

pushed it into her hand. She tried to give it back to him. 'I don't want this.'

'Listen ma'am. I'm going to try flushing him out of the porch. Soon as your way's clear you run like a scared cat through that door, and try holding up the ceremony. Just point the gun and act like you mean it.'

The man in the doorway was just lolling there, soaking up the sunshine, and not fretting about anything in particular. 'Right, ma'am,' Henry muttered, 'When I get hold of you just start kicking and screaming. Like I was hurting you real bad.'

'What in Hanover do you mean, Henry Deacon?'

There was no more time for explanations. Clenching his hands on her shoulders he started to shake her furiously. 'This is all your fault, you addle-headed old woman! I go out for five minutes and this happens. You've got no more sense than you were born with!'

She got the idea quick enough. A couple of startled birds wheeled away from the branches above them as she blasted off with an aggrieved screech. 'Let me go. You're hurting me. You stop it.' Struggling, she let fly a blistering kick, which connected with his calf and Henry winced with real pain.

'You asked for it now!' Knotting his fist, he started to raise his hand, and then there was a roar of protest from the man in the porch.

'I told you, mister. Nobody treats a lady like that!' He came lumbering towards them; he wasn't a man built for speed, either in movement, or thinking. 'It don't matter what she's done, you treat her nicely ...'

'Right, ma'am, just get in there!'

She broke away from Henry, picked up her skirts, and went hurtling off past the bemused sentry.

'Hey where you going?'

Then all the breath slammed out of him as Henry shoulder charged him. As Henry bounced away, Barney gasped, pulling in a painful couple of lungfuls of air, and then bellowed in anger, heaving a meaty paw in a massive arc. If Henry hadn't ducked, his head would likely have followed Mrs Peacock all the way into the house. He straightened and fired a right into the other man's midriff. It was about as much fun as punching a tree, and had about as much effect.

'You need teaching a lesson, mister! I've known Mis' Peacock since I was knee-high. Nobody's gonna treat her like that while I'm around!'

Henry sidestepped again, but this time the roundhouse swing caught him bruisingly on the shoulder and sent him stumbling. Mrs Peacock was inside the house now, and he decided this distraction had gone on long enough. Barney's concern for his fellow human beings was strictly restricted to members of the opposite sex, and he sensed that he was in danger of being more than a touch damaged.

The massive hands caught hold of his coat, yanking him back. 'Just turn round and face me like a man!'

'Another time, maybe!' yelled Henry as he slid out of his coat and threw himself towards the house. He could feel the ground shaking as Barney pursued him, but he got to the door first, dived inside, and slammed it shut, shooting the bolt across.

It took a moment for his eyes to adjust to the dimmer light in here, and then he saw an open door down at the end of the long hallway. Barney was now hammering on the door, but Henry ignored him and dashed down the hallway.

'You took your time,' observed Mrs Peacock, as he came into the wood-panelled room.

He grabbed the revolver from her, still breathless. Mathilda sat on a chair, pale-faced, just staring ahead of her. Close by her stood a man wearing a shapeless buffalo coat. He was about five feet tall, with a broken beaver hat perched on his bony bald head. 'What in hell's name you and this woman playing at, mister?' he wheezed in a reedy voice. His withered, sunk-in face had a petulant look to it. 'Hell'n damnation. We was almost done with. Just waiting for her to say her words. Breaking up a feller's wedding it's against the law. Ain't it, judge?'

'You're Hiram Gliss?' Henry shook his head in undisguised disgust. 'You can't go ahead with marrying this feller, Mathilda!'

He got no response from her, and now Blackitt took a couple of steps forward, his flabby face quivering. 'She's marrying him, Deacon. She's got a legal agreement with him. You holding a gun on us don't make no difference to that. I knew we'd have trouble with you, Deacon. Right off, I did.'

He scowled, 'Hell, can someone go tell Bates to stop hammering on that blasted door before he smashes it in.' He half turned, 'Mellick, you go tell him!'

The other man in the room was cowering back against the wall. He was a skinny, scruffy individual. 'I ain't going nowhere judge. I only come as a witness to this wedding. I don't wanna get shot.'

'You want to carry on being court clerk,' barked Blackitt, 'You'll do as you're damn well told!'

'Please put the gun away, Henry.' Mathilda spoke for the first time. 'I don't want anyone to get hurt.'

'First bit of sense anyone's spoken,' said Mrs Peacock. 'Just everyone calm down. And I'll go'n tell Barney to stop punching holes in the door.'

Reluctantly, Henry slammed the gun back into its holster, and she hurried off down the hall.

Blackitt pulled out his red bandanna, shook his bulging head, and wiped his neck. 'You're acting like a crazy man, Deacon. There ain't nothing illegal about this wedding. Nobody's forcing the lady to marry Hiram.'

Gliss jabbed a finger in Mathilda's direction. 'I can't figure what your angle is, mister, but this gal done made a promise to marry me. If she don't, then that uncle o' hers is going to be hearing from me.' The old man bared his blackened teeth in a grotesque parody of a smile. 'Life ain't going to be so rosy for him. Or his missus.'

Henry heard Mrs Peacock's voice down the hallway, calming Barney Bates down, but he kept looking at Mathilda. 'You don't owe them anything. They had no right to marry you off to … him.'

'It's either the gal marries me, or her uncle loses his house and his business. That's the deal.'

Mathilda shook her head hopelessly. 'I don't care about my uncle, but my aunt, she's not a well woman. She was kind to me. If she lost her house …'

Gliss glowered. 'Well, that's how it is. Life's going to be tough for a lot of folk if we don't get this matter settled. And I want it settled quick.'

He moved towards Mathilda, and she shrank back at his approach. 'You better make up your mind, gal,' he threatened in that high-pitched voice. 'You marry me, and you and your kin'll be just dandy. I got a real fine place waiting for you up in Diamond Rock.'

Mrs Peacock came back. She had Henry's jacket

over her arm. 'Now, have you men made your minds up what's to be done? 'Cause as far as I'm concerned, Mathilda's not marrying him.' She hurled a blistering look at Gliss. 'You'd got no right to come dragging her outa my house, mister. I need to have a proper talk with her.'

'I don't have any choice, Mrs Peacock.' Mathilda spoke in a dull, lifeless voice.

'There y'are then,' snapped Gliss triumphantly. 'C'mon Luther Blackitt, you get this ceremony done with, so I can get about my business.'

Henry stood there uncertainly. A whole dazzle of thoughts whirled round his head, as deafening as a crowd of seagulls circling over a fishing boat in 'Frisco Bay. Mathilda was alone, and helpless; just like his brother had been. It didn't matter what she said, or did. Maybe she could stay and work for Mrs Peacock, but Gliss wouldn't let her be. He was the kind of mean-minded, vicious feller who'd never leave anything alone while he had a chance to get what he wanted.

The words were out before he even had time to think about them. 'She's going to marry me, that's what! Then this old buzzard won't be able to bother her.'

'You keep your britches on, boy!' howled Gliss. 'This one ain't smoothing your sheets!'

Mathilda was staring in disbelief. 'Henry, don't be foolish. You can't marry me. We only met yesterday.'

'Then you've known me twice as long as you've known this old buzzard.'

Gliss let out another roar. 'She's marrying me. Else her folks'll be looking for a roof over their heads this winter.'

'I'll make sure your aunt doesn't suffer too bad,' gabbled Henry. 'Guess your uncle can take his own chances, but if it comes to it, she can come live in California. I still got my father's house back there.'

Mathilda was wide-eyed in astonishment. 'Why're you doing this, Henry? You can't. You don't owe me anything.'

'You don't have to marry me,' he said quickly, 'Not if you don't want to. Heck, I'm not forcing you.'

She got slowly to her feet. 'I guess I need to talk to Henry. In private. So I'd be obliged if the rest of you could leave us alone.'

Mellick, Blackitt's clerk, was on his grateful way almost before her words were out. Mrs Peacock thrust Henry's jacket at him, and fired a look at Gliss and Blackitt. 'I reckon you owe her that much.'

'I'm still marrying her!' retorted Gliss, but he shuffled towards the door. He turned as he reached it, 'You just come to your senses, gal, you hear!'

Blackitt glowered at Henry. 'I thought you come to Charity on your murdering brother's account, Deacon. Seems to me you don't rightly know what you want.'

The door slammed shut, and Mathilda stared at him for a long moment. Henry's head was still buzzing from the offer he'd made. It had seemed the only way out at the time, but there was certainly no gratitude in those grey eyes. There was something changed about her all of a sudden; the fear and hopelessness had gone.

Still watching him close as a hawk, she folded her arms. At last she spoke, 'Well, Mr Deacon, I suppose you think you've been real clever? Real gallant, saving a lady from a fate worse than death.'

This was a different woman all of a sudden. For

most of the time he'd known Mathilda Farnell, she'd been like a scared rabbit, the kind who'd jump at every noise, who'd burst into tears at the slightest thing. 'I only did what I reckoned was right ...' he began falteringly.

'Is that so?' The corners of her mouth twitched in a humourless smile. 'Maybe you'd like to try explaining that to my bosses up in Washington.'

'What in hell are you talking about?'

'Attorney-General's Department, Henry. I'm out here on government business.'

Henry gaped. 'Oh sure! You're a Federal Marshal. First time I ever heard of them giving that kind of job to a woman.'

'They say there's a first time for everything,' she returned evenly. 'You calling me a liar?'

Shaking his head, he mumbled that he wasn't doing that. This was crazy, impossible; yet something told him Mathilda was telling him the truth. 'So you're saying that the US government's sent you out here to marry that stinking bag of bones? Why in hell would they do that?'

'I've told you as much as I can, Henry.'

'You sure fooled me,' he said. 'All those tears at the way station. You must be able to turn them on like a faucet.' Another thought struck him, 'So you're not really Mathilda Farnell, then?'

She shrugged, and Henry realised he'd been given all he was going to get. Still, he was determined to carry on trying. As he started to say something else, though, the door behind him was shoved open sharply.

Swinging round, he saw Judge Blackitt. 'Wedding's been postponed till noon. Hiram had some business to do down at the Paradise. Figured he'd get that outa the way while you and Deacon was passing the time of day with each other. So you two can take yourself off somewhere else to talk.'

Mathilda slipped back into her other personality as easily as putting on her shawl. Her shoulders slumped, and all the colour seemed to have drained from her face. Her lips quivered, 'I didn't mean to cause you any trouble, judge. Mr Deacon was only trying to help me.'

'Like I say he'll be back here at noon,' Blackitt's piggy eyes screwed up as he grinned coarsely, 'We'll get this wedding finished off, then you can go on your honeymoon. He'll take care o' you. In all sorts of ways. He may be old, but there's still a fire burning in there somewhere.'

Henry flinched, 'You'd be happy to see a daughter of yours marrying that man, Blackitt?'

'I ain't got no kids, mister. Best way.' He ladled a good helping of menace into his voice. 'Once this lady's on her way, maybe you oughta think about buying yourself a ticket outa here, Deacon. Hear you had a set-to with young Dan Finnegan.'

'Seems you've been spreading the word about me arriving in Charity,' commented Henry sourly.

'Well you sure as hell wasn't going to keep it secret, boy. You was lucky with Dan this time. Next time it could be you'd get filled so full of lead that it'll take six men and a brace of horses to drag your carcase to the cemetery.'

'You're real good at making threats, judge,' Henry shot back swiftly. 'They'll come back on you, one day.'

'Well, the way you're going on, you won't be round to see that day,' countered Blackitt. 'Now you take your lady friend outa here, but just you make damn sure she's back here at noon.' He strode out of the room.

Mathilda looked at Henry. 'I'm coming back here, Henry. Nothing'll stop me.'

Right now, he was lost for words. He followed her down the hall. Mrs Peacock was waiting outside for them, watching down towards where Gliss was wheeling his wagon team round so he could take the rig back into town. Judge Blackitt was waddling down the hill towards him, puffing and panting with the exertion.

Barney Bates stood by the oak tree, and glowered as Henry came out. Mrs Peacock shot him a warning glance. 'You mind your manners, Barney. And it's time you found yourself a decent feller to work for. One day Judge Blackitt'll fall into a deep, dark hole, and maybe you'll fall in with him!'

She turned to look at Henry. 'You got this one to change her mind?'

'I've done my best,' he said in a low voice. 'But she still seems set on it.'

'What choice do I have?' muttered Mathilda, and Henry marvelled again at just how convincing all her play-acting was. They set off down the hill, and something made him glance back at the house. The drapes at an upstairs window flickered, and he saw someone watching them. A woman, he reckoned, though she moved out of his view as soon as she knew he'd spotted her.

'Judge got a wife, has he?'

Mrs Peacock sniffed disapprovingly. 'She kept herself outa the way, didn't she? And no, she ain't his wife. Used to be one of the girls at the Paradise. Now she lives with him. Another one who'll go down when he does, and that's for sure.'

Once more she turned her attention to Mathilda. 'You could do worse than marry this feller. Go live in California. Get some colour back in those pretty cheeks of yours.'

The idea put a glow on her own face as she carried on down the hill ahead of them. No doubt Mrs Peacock was as tough as old leather, but there was a broad seam of sentiment running through her as well. Henry and Mathilda walked side by side, not speaking.

They reached the house, and Mrs Peacock turned in the doorway. 'Now, I got myself some things to do. You two young folks just set down here, and do some hard talking, you hear?'

Once the other woman was safely out of earshot, Mathilda said, keeping her voice low, 'What I told you back there, Henry, you're not to tell anyone else. I hope I can trust you.'

Looking hard into those grey eyes, he squared his chin. 'You sure you can trust these bosses of yours? They must be crazy sending a lone woman into a place like Diamond Rock. Some kind of spying work is it? From what I've read of that profession the survival rate is none too generous.'

He lowered his voice, 'And have they really given you orders to marry Gliss? Hell, are they expecting you to …?' Unable to bring himself to say the words, he just went silent at the thought of it.

Mathilda had listened to him impassively enough, but she gave a shiver. 'Henry, there's a part of me would sooner die than let Hiram Gliss touch me. Another part of me says that him and his kind will never be brought low if folk don't make sacrifices.'

He snatched at the words. 'Him and his kind? So

he's up to some real wickedness up in Diamond Rock, then?'

'You won't get me to tell you,' she replied doggedly. 'The less anyone knows about this, the better. It's the only way.'

'But maybe I could help you!'

Mathilda reached out and touched his cheek. 'Just you stop worrying about me. You just take care of yourself. Now, I think I'll go to my room. Pack my things away.' A faint smile played on her lips. 'It was real sweet of you to offer to marry me. I could do a lot worse, like Mrs Peacock says.'

'And you are doing a lot worse. A hundred times worse,' said Henry helplessly. 'This is crazy, Mathilda.'

He let her go with a defeated sigh, and paced out onto the road, staring down the hill. Then he saw a skinny, dark-garbed figure loping up in his direction. It was Mellick, Judge Blackitt's pasty-faced clerk. The man stopped nervously as he reached Henry. 'You just leave your gun in its holster, mister,' he bleated.

'You carry on up to your boss's house, Mellick. You're not worth the price of a bullet.'

Mellick shook his head. 'Judge Blackitt sent me up from the Paradise.'

'Wants to hold the wedding down there, does he?' asked Henry bitterly. 'Hell, why not? Might be even more fitting to hold it out in the cemetery. That feller Gliss smells like something that died a week ago.'

'There won't be no wedding today,' Mellick cut in. 'That's what I'm to tell the lady.'

Henry gave a long whistle. 'A burying, then?' he asked hopefully, 'Gliss finally decided he was dead?'

'Will you quit confusing me!' snapped Mellick unhappily. 'He had to go back to Diamond Rock unexpected. Couple of his boys came riding in a few minutes back. He just climbed aboard his wagon and took himself off.'

A spasm of relief shivered through Henry. 'When is he coming back?'

The court clerk shrugged, 'I don't rightly know.' He tried to look dignified, 'Anyways, I gotta tell the lady that she's to move into the judge's house till Mr Gliss gets back. So he can keep an eye on her.'

'Is that so?' He moved to one side, 'Well, you go tell that to Mrs Peacock, Mellick. I'm sure she'll be glad to hear those tidings.'

Mellick stared nervously towards the open door of the house. 'I figure you can tell her as well as me, Deacon. I got things to do.'

Henry was already moving off down the hill. 'So've I.' It'd be real fun to watch Mrs Peacock's reaction when Mellick told her that Mathilda had to go live with the judge. But there was no sense in risking getting caught in the crossfire.

He whistled a jaunty tune as he strode down the hill towards town. Maybe this was just delaying the inevitable, but while Mathilda stayed in Charity, there was still hope that the wedding would never take place. And that mattered to him more than he was going to admit to anyone, yet. But now Mathilda's problem was just simmering on the back-burner, it was time he started trying to make some headway with his own mission.

FIVE

'This is all your fault,' Mathilda hissed at Henry as they stood in the dim light of the narrow upstairs landing.

'I don't figure it is exactly,' he retorted. 'Mrs Peacock was as anxious as me to stop you getting married to that walking dung-heap.'

'Sure, but without you she'd never have got into the house.' She turned away from him, peering through the slats of the window blind. 'There's no telling how long it might be before Gliss comes back to Charity.'

Henry moved to her shoulder. 'And maybe that's for the best. You just wire ... whoever you need to tell. Get them to come up with another crazy plan.'

Mathilda twisted round sharply and their faces almost touched. 'You don't know what you're talking about Henry. I won't get another chance!'

Her sweet-smelling perfume wafted over him, and unwillingly, Henry stepped back. 'I'm still not sorry, Mathilda. Can't say I am.'

'No?' She shook her head, 'And suppose I got in the way of your ... mission to find out what happened to your brother. You figure that's important, don't you?'

'Yeah, but ...'

'But nothing!' she snapped, 'I'm sure he was a good man, didn't deserve what happened to him. But just one man. I'm worried about a whole lot more people.'

'If you'd tell me ...'

But she pushed past him, and went into her room, shutting the door noisily behind her. Henry stood there a moment. He tried to feel remorse for skewing up things for her, but he just couldn't. All he knew was that she'd been saved from riding back to Diamond Rock to face a life with Hiram Gliss. Federal marshal or not, she was still a woman, and he wouldn't wish that on any woman.

He began to go downstairs, and as he reached the bottom, Vinny Peacock clattered in, with an important air about him. 'Things are getting real bad in this territory, Mr Deacon, and that's a fact!'

'Is it now, Vinny?'

The boy's mother came out of the kitchen, wiping her floury hands on her apron. 'What you doing back home, son? They closed the depot early? Or have you got fired for some foolishness?'

'I ain't got fired, mom,' he said scathingly. 'Just figured you'd want to hear the news. Mail stage just got in. The Arizona Devils have raided the Farmers' Bank over in Benson.'

'Dear God,' she exclaimed nervously, 'That's getting too close for comfort.'

'Sure is,' Vinny agreed. His self-important manner faltered a little. 'It was real bad this time, mom. There was four ladies in there. Mother and three daughters.'

Mrs Peacock's hand went to her mouth. 'They got harmed, did they?'

'Dead,' muttered Vinny. 'All of them. One of the

tellers pulled a gun it seemed, and those bast … those buzzards just blasted off at everyone in the bank. A feller who came in on the stage saw 'em riding out. Says he swears they was all laughing fit to bust their wicked britches.'

His mother shook her head in disbelief. 'Sometimes, I start to wonder whether Almighty God ain't got His back turned on us folk out here. Four women …' She swung round and went slowly back to her kitchen.

Henry stared at Vinny, thinking of the grief in his own household when Lew's dead body arrived back. That woman in Benson doubtless had a husband; father to three girls. A shaft of painful pity went through him as he thought of that man's agony. 'Time somebody did something,' he muttered.

There was a creak on the stairway, and he turned and looked up to see Mathilda standing there. She'd clearly heard Vinny's news; and her face was as pale as Mrs Peacock's had been. But she was staring squarely into Henry's face, and her eyes blazed with what he knew was accusation.

'Mathilda …' He started up the stairs towards her, but she immediately retreated into her room, and he turned back, with some kind of realisation growing in him. She'd been sent out here because of those cold-hearted devil riders. He couldn't imagine just how marrying Hiram Gliss might fit in with that, but he knew that was the truth. The message in those burning eyes was as clear as if she'd spoken: *A whole lot more innocent men and women might die, Henry Deacon, because you decided to act like some kind of knight in shining armour!*

'Bad business, Mr Deacon,' said Vinny.

'And that's the truth,' Henry mumbled.

'Take some more apple pie, Henry,' urged Mrs Peacock. 'You look like a man could do with some energy.'

'If he don't want it, mom,' Vinny declared, 'I'll finish it off.'

'He's paying for his meal,' she reminded her son. 'You ain't!'

'I guess I'm not real hungry,' said Henry apologetically. All through supper he'd been aware of Mathilda sitting there, her resentment simmering about how he'd interfered. She was respectful enough when anyone spoke to her, but Henry didn't doubt that Mrs Peacock could read her mood as well as he could.

Vinny, on the other hand, was oblivious to anything but the slice of pie he was easing onto his plate. He suddenly realised that everyone else was watching him. 'Anyone else want some?' he asked uncertainly, his spoon poised midway between his plate and his mouth.

'Oh, just get it eaten, Vinny,' said his mother wearily. 'Though where all the food goes in that skinny frame of yours I just don't know. Just disappears. Mind, your pa was much the same.'

Glad to have something else to talk about, Henry inquired carefully, 'I guess you'll be a widow, Mrs Peacock?'

'Seven, nearly eight years,' she told him. 'George Peacock was a good man. But he got the wanderlust now and then. Like most men, I guess.'

'My brother for one,' Henry commented softly.

'Sure.' The woman blinked a couple of times. 'Like your brother. And Vinny's pa ended up getting killed because he couldn't stop his boots a-wandering off with him now'n then.'

'How was that?' queried Mathilda, taking a genuine interest in something for the first time this evening.

'He went in search o' silver. Like so many of 'em. Bought himself a mule and a bedroll, a parcel of tools and him and half a dozen others rode out to the Chiricahuas.'

She smiled affectionately at her son, who was doing his own mining operation in the piece of pie on his plate. 'That one there wanted to go with 'em. His pa had the sense not to let him.'

Pressing her hands together hard, she paused. Though she was telling this casually enough, it was plain that deep down it still hurt some. 'Anyhow, the rest of them rode back in not much more'n a month. The weather had been real wet up there that month. Real miserable up on the high ridges. They'd been camping out in a steep canyon, close to a fast-running stream. George took it into his head to do some fishing.'

Vinny looked up. 'They'd run clean outa food, mom. That's why he done that.'

'Sure,' she agreed. 'That's why he decided to do it. But it was raining, the rocks themselves were as slippy as fish. Nobody saw him fall. They found him two miles downstream, caught up in a tangle of brushwood. Not a mark on him maybe, but he was dead just the same.'

Standing up sharply, she set to gathering the supper plates together. 'They buried him out there. I tell you, when I finally get to see him again, like I will one day ... well, he'll get a real bawling-out from me!'

Her son waved his spoon at her. 'You don't mean that, mom! Pa was only trying to help his pals. If a man's going to die, maybe it's better he dies trying doing something good.'

Mrs Peacock shook her head fiercely, and reached for Vinny's plate. 'I'd sooner he hadn't needed to try fishing in Skull Canyon. He might still ...'

'Skull Canyon?'

Mathilda and Henry had both blurted out the words at once; so close together you couldn't have separated them with a fine-bladed knife. They stared at each other in a mixture of surprise and confusion. Mathilda recovered her composure first, and gave a little toss of her head. 'Sounds a grim sort of name. Skull Canyon. That's all I was going to say.'

Like hell you were, thought Henry, but he nodded briskly. 'Me too. Seems though the both of us think alike, Mrs Peacock.'

'Guess you do,' she concurred. 'And I'd say that if a young man and a young woman get that close to sharing their thoughts, then it'd be a crying shame for them not to get wed.'

'Let me help you with those plates,' said Mathilda quickly, avoiding Henry's gaze.

The other woman waved the offer away. 'Won't hear of it, Mathilda. You stay there.' She turned her eyes on her son. 'Vinny?'

He looked expectantly at her. 'Yes mom?'

'Run down to Vernon's Store and fetch me some washing soda.'

'Now, mom? Heck, can't it wait till morning? Not doing any laundry now, are you?'

'Just do it!' she snapped.

Henry saw what the point was. She was determined to leave him and Mathilda sitting together alone in the dining room. He wasn't so sure that was one of her best ideas. 'Maybe I could go with him.'

'No, you stay there, too. You'll just get indigestion, Henry, if you rush off.'

Vinny hitched up his levis. 'And how about me?' he complained sourly.

His mother glowered. 'You never have that trouble! Now you shift yourself real sharp. And come straight back. No peering into the Paradise, you hear?'

'There's plenty of fellers my age go drinking in there!'

'So there is,' she acknowledged, 'But while you're living under this roof Vincent Peacock, you'll stay away from strong liquor and hard-faced women.'

Vinny went his way, and she went hers, and Mathilda and Henry stared at each other. 'Quite a woman, Mrs P,' he remarked. 'She's got Vinny under her thumb.'

Her grey eyes narrowed, 'Which is where he wants to be, I'd say. She looks after him, feeds him, washes his clothes. Why should he risk that for ...?'

'Liquor and women? Plenty do.'

'What do you know about Skull Canyon?' she asked abruptly.

'It's where Mrs Peacock's husband drowned,' he answered evenly. 'What do you know about it?'

'I asked first.'

'We could go on like that all night,' he said. 'I know you're real sore at me. And after what happened in Benson today, maybe you've got reason. You being here is something to do with that gang, isn't it?'

'You tell me what you know about Skull Canyon,' Mathilda insisted stubbornly. 'You've certainly heard of it before. Your ears twitched like a jack-rabbit's when Mrs Peacock mentioned it.'

Henry laughed. 'They twitched? My ears?'

Allowing her face to unfreeze a touch, she smiled faintly. 'If they could have, they would.' Then she leaned forward urgently, 'Please, Henry. Just tell me.'

'I don't really know anything about it,' he said. 'Except that Lew talked about it in the last letter he sent home. He was in Phoenix. Buying tools, supplies, something, I suppose. Told us he'd been prospecting deep in the mountains. In a place called Skull Canyon.'

'Nothing else?'

Henry shrugged. 'It was plain as pumpkin stew that Lew thought he was going to make himself a rich man. There was silver to be found, he wrote, and he was damn well going to find it!' He broke off a moment. 'Anyway, next thing we heard, Lew wasn't rich. He was just dead.'

'Do you think he did go back to Skull Canyon?'

'Mathilda Farnell, or whatever your name is, I don't know what the hell my brother did. That's why I came all the way out here to Charity.' He bristled a little. 'I know as much about the last weeks of my brother's life as I know about you. Maybe even less, and that's sure saying something!'

She kept her voice very low. 'Skull Canyon's a very lonely place, Henry, from what I hear. Up above Diamond Rock.'

'Yeah?' He watched her hard. She wasn't so much talking to him as thinking aloud.

'Cuts deep and high into the mountains.' Mathilda gazed down at the old dining table, folding her hands together like she was praying. 'Perched up there a man could look down on Diamond Rock and get a good look at what was going on there. Sam McWheel says …'

Suddenly snapping out of her day-dream, she stared at him in round-eyed alarm. 'Just forget I said anything, Henry.'

'Who in hell is Sam McWheel?' he demanded.

Mathilda shook her head fiercely. 'Henry you don't want to get involved!'

'I am involved!' Reaching across the table, he grabbed one of her hands. 'Let's just say Lew was up there near Skull Canyon, Mathilda. Let's say he saw something that made him quit the mountains and ride back into town. Soon as he got here, someone saw to it that his mouth was closed for ever. Then let's just try fitting all those things together, shall we?'

'What do you mean?' she stammered, trying to pull her hand away from his firm grip.

'You're the government agent, Mathilda. You tell me. Being a simple kind of feller, when it comes to it, I'd say that maybe we're both trying to peer over the same wall.'

At last she pulled her hand free of his fingers. 'I've never heard of your brother, Henry. Whatever happened to him can't have anything to do with …'

'With why you're here?' he demanded, 'And why not? S'pose … s'pose Lew saw a gang of fellers riding into Diamond Rock. Dozen men on big horses, maybe.'

'You don't know that, do you?'

He felt a little quiver of triumph at the unease in her voice. 'No, but I got a good idea.'

Mathilda looked back at him miserably. 'I shouldn't be talking to you about any of this, Henry.' She listened for a moment to Mrs Peacock clattering round in the kitchen on the other side of the dining room wall. 'Especially where someone might hear us.'

'Fair enough,' Henry said, 'Well, I tell you how we get some kind of privacy, Mathilda. I'm taking a ride out tomorrow. Paying a call on someone who might just be able to throw a light on what happened to Lew. Maybe you should ride out with me.'

'I'll think about it.' She pushed herself to her feet. 'I really will, I promise.'

Henry heard her join Mrs Peacock in the kitchen. Something told him that she would be joining him on his trip out to Marty Wilson's homestead. He yawned, and scratched his chin. It had been a long, troubling day. He'd turn in early tonight, a visit to the Paradise Saloon would have to wait for another time. Old Chet Stookey had demanded that Henry get him a certain racy souvenir.

'I don't blame you for selling the business and making me retire, young Henry!' he'd declared, 'But I figure I'm due some favour for teaching you to shoot straight. And I want a frilly garter still warm from the legs of one of the gals that work in that there Paradise Saloon. Something like that'll make my retirement a whole lot more pleasureable!'

With a grin at the memory of Chet's request, Henry strolled out into the night air, and looked up at the moon hanging there like a juicy slice of melon, and the sky-parade of hat-sized stars. The sound of piano playing tinnily floated up from the town, and a burst of laughter came from somewhere. He sniffed; you could almost smell the whisky and tobacco fumes drifting up with the noise.

Glad to be out in the open, he sauntered up the hill, hands in his britches pockets. One day, maybe the whole of Charity would be as quiet and peaceful as it was up here. Maybe that was the kind of thing that Mathilda's bosses were aiming for. 'Course, there'd always be bad men. That was human nature. But you didn't have to make things easy for them. Out here it was still too simple for a man to build an empire built on power and fear. Someone like Judge Luther Blackitt, for instance. He wore the cloak of his legal standing as a shield against his corruption. As he thought of Blackitt, Henry realised that he'd almost reached the place where he'd challenged Barney Bates this morning. There was no light glowing in any window of the judge's house, and it had a gloomy, abandoned look about it.

'Just like it will for real one day,' Henry said aloud, stopping a few yards from the dark shape of that old oak tree.

'Wouldn't have put you down as a man who talked to himself.'

For a moment he stared in bewilderment at the tree which seemed to have spoken to him. Then she came round from behind it, and let out a giggle. 'Did I scare you, soldier?'

'No ma'am,' he stuttered. 'And I'm no soldier.'

The woman approached him. She was wearing a black, tight-fitting dress, which stretched across the proud curve of her breasts, and dark ringlets fell across her bare white shoulders which gleamed like marble in the moonlight. He'd seen a drawing in the *Police Gazette* once which looked a lot like this woman. It had been with a story of a countess from Italy or some other place in Europe who'd beguiled a whole bunch of young bloods into her palace and then murdered them for pleasure.

'Saw you tussling with that big hulk this morning.' There was a purring admiration in her voice which both unnerved and fascinated him. Then he came to his senses, and took a closer look at her. Sure, she was wearing the kind of powerful scent which turned a man's soul to jelly, but as she neared him, his nose recognised another perfume, that of whisky. She'd been drinking, and she was none too steady on her feet.

Taking a breath, he said, 'I guess you must be the judge's ...' He broke off, embarrassed, remembering what Mrs Peacock had said about the woman who lived with Blackitt.

'Yup,' she agreed, 'I'm the judge's. Period! Though he don't spend a lot of time with me, soldier.' She was reaching out a hand to him, and he decided it was time he scuffed up some dust.

'Been nice meeting you, ma'am, but ...'

'My name's Juliet.' He hadn't moved quick enough, and long fingers caught at his sleeve. 'What do they call you, soldier?'

'I'm Henry. And I do have to go, ma'am. I'm sorry.'

'No you don't,' she told him firmly, and she put her hands on his shoulders and pressed herself into him, and tried to kiss him.

'Listen, ma'am,' he eased her back with a gentle

push, 'I'd say you'd be best getting inside, and ... getting some sleep. Which is what I'm set on doing.'

She was swaying slightly as she stood there, and with a shock he realised that tears were trickling down her cheeks. 'You think I'm ugly, don't you? Luther thinks I'm ugly. He must do. Spends all his time down at the Paradise with girls I used to work with.'

'I don't think you're ugly, ma'am,' gabbled Henry. 'But I figure it's best I don't start getting involved with things that aren't my concern. You see, I'm a stranger here, and ...'

Juliet wiped at her tears with both hands, smearing her rouge and powder. 'Your brother was a stranger, too.'

'What did you say?'

Turning away from him, she began walking unsteadily back to the house. Henry caught up with her. 'You know something about my brother, Miss Juliet?'

'Just come in with me a minute, soldier,' she said. 'Have a drink, and maybe we'll talk. Or whatever else you feel like doing.' As she entered the porchway, she swung round, and stood facing him, hands on hips. 'Luther he's not in, so you needn't be feared. There's just me. Just little me.'

Juliet carried on into the house, and Henry stayed where he was, torn with indecision. If Blackitt found him here, he could be in all sorts of trouble. But this woman knew that he was Lew Deacon's brother. It didn't necessarily mean she'd be able to tell him anything about Lew's time in Charity that he didn't already know. But she lived with Judge Blackitt, and so there was just a chance he might find out something from her.

So, uneasily, he followed her, and came into the wide living room off the hallway just in time to stop her tipping over an oil lamp she'd just lighted. 'You let me do that, ma'am.'

She curled herself on a plush chaise longue, and watched as he lit the lamps, sending a warm yellow glow all round the room. 'Lucky you came by, Henry. Come sit here, next to me.'

'Maybe I should make you some coffee, or something?'

'I only drink coffee in the morning.' She pushed her hair back from her face. 'If you're still here in the morning, I'll take you up on that offer.' Her smile was inviting, 'Luther often stays out all night. Like some old tom-cat.'

Henry stayed on his feet. 'You know something about my brother Lew?'

There was a flicker of impatience in her dark eyes. 'All this talk, Henry.' She slapped a hand on the seat beside her. 'You come sit here. Keep me company, else I won't tell you nothing.' There was the tone of a spoiled child in that little outburst, but it had also had the effect of sobering her up a little.

He came and sat down next to her, but she made no attempt to touch him, not even looking at him for a moment or two. 'You put one over on Luther and that stink-bag Hiram Gliss today. He was real mad, Henry. Not often he doesn't get his own way.' Now she did look at him, 'But that little girl's a mouse. You could do a lot better for yourself. With a real woman …'

Her hand strayed onto his shoulder, and slid up his neck. 'You got real nice hair, Henry. Clean. Kind of soft.'

There was no doubting that her touch sent a

tingle through him. Another time, another place, he'd likely start doing all the things his father had once warned him against. 'Did you ever meet my brother?'

Juliet pulled her hand away. 'Your brother's dead, Henry. Worrying about him won't bring him back.'

'I said, did you ever meet him?'

Sitting up straight, she folded her arms across her bosom. 'I saw him. Not to talk to. I was watching from window upstairs. Saw him come up the hill with one of Luther's drinking chums from the Paradise.'

He stared at her in dumb incredulity. 'Lew was here, in this house?'

'I don't figure he stayed long. Arrived about noon, left maybe fifteen minutes later. All in one piece. Next thing I heard, he'd had a set to with Stretch Finnegan in an alley off Main Street, and was in the lock-up.' She stood up, 'I need another drink.'

There was a bottle and some glasses on an ornate sideboard in the corner. She poured herself a hefty measure. 'You care for one? It's real good bourbon. Not like the poison Gliss sold to the Apaches.' She laughed, 'They'll get even with that buzzard one day for that.'

He frowned, baffled. 'You're saying Hiram Gliss trades with the Apaches?'

'You don't know much, do you soldier? He'll take dollars from anyone. US or Mexican. Had himself a couple crates of bad whisky. They say a miner up in Diamond Rock died from drinking it. So he sold it off to his Indian friends.'

'How do you know all this, Juliet?' He shook his

head. This wasn't what he wanted to talk about. 'Did the judge tell you what my brother wanted to talk about?'

'Nope.' She downed most of the whisky in one swallow, and her eyes glinted. 'Do I get some reward now, for telling you that?'

'You haven't told me much.' Henry got to his feet. 'And my mother used to say that honesty was its own reward.'

'Honesty?' Juliet finished the rest of the whisky. 'That's a foreign country to most folk round here.' Picking up the bottle again, she refilled her glass. 'So I guess you prefer that whey-faced mouse to me, do you? Hell, there can't be much blood running in her tight little veins, if she's willing to let her uncle marry her off to Hiram Gliss. I wouldn't let no man treat me like that.'

He was moving towards the door. 'So how come you're living with Blackitt, then?'

She ignored that question, and began to move in his direction, grabbing at him. 'Don't go. Just stay a little while longer. I won't try dragging you into bed or nothing. I just get so damn lonely up here.'

He tried to shake her hand off his arm, pushing her back, and hoping there was nobody watching this through the undraped window. 'Look, I'm grateful for what you told me, Juliet. Might be better you didn't tell the judge I was here. And it might be better for you if you got yourself out of this house.'

She glowered, and came right up to him. There was an ugly twist to her face now. 'What in hell do you know 'bout it?' she shouted.

'Just calm down.' He eased her back again.

'You're a man, you go where you choose, do

what you choose. I got to make the best of what little I have. Luther might throw me out one day, but till he does, I'm staying put!'

Now she twisted away from him, and slumped down on the chaise longue, her head lolling back. The drink was taking over again, and she'd soon fall asleep.

Henry looked down at her, and then took himself out, hurrying away from the house. Maybe he should have tried her with more questions, but he was glad to be out of there. He looked towards the gas-lit glare of the town where Lewis Deacon had died. He'd learned just a little more today, like when you turned a corner and saw a different part of the view.

Back in the Turkey Springs Way Station, Luther Blackitt had told him a deliberate lie. Said that the first time he'd clapped eyes on Lewis Deacon was when they dragged him into the courtroom. Now he knew that wasn't true. For some reason Lew had called on the very same man who only the next day had sentenced him to dangle from a rope.

He set his shoulders square, and a grim, hollow laugh rolled round inside him. Well, he'd seen his first hanging judge here in Charity. Maybe it wouldn't be too long before he saw his first judge hanging!

SIX

Henry and Mathilda didn't do much talking until they'd left Charity a good few miles behind them. As he'd expected, she'd agreed to come with him out to the homestead owned by Marty Wilson, the deputy who'd felt enough common decency to go in search of someone to defend Lewis Deacon. But the prospect seemed to give her no pleasure, as she sat next to him on the cushioned seat of the rig he'd picked up from the livery first thing that morning.

She'd been tight-lipped and silent ever since they'd turned onto the well marked, deep-rutted prospectors' trail out towards the mountain. Maybe she was recalling that if he hadn't interrupted proceedings back at Blackitt's house then she would have ridden this way yesterday, sitting with her foul-mouthed, ill-smelling new husband, instead of next to him.

Anyway, he was in no hurry to talk. They had all day, and Mrs Peacock had told them that if time ran too late, then they were to stay over at the Wilsons' place until the next day.

'She'll make you real welcome, I know, will Shirley-May. She's a real friendly, hard-working girl. And I guess she'll be glad of some company, too.' She'd frowned, 'She and Marty, they've taken on a hard life all the way out there. Horse-rearing, I heard.'

Vinny, finishing his breakfast, had butted in earnestly, 'But just you keep an eye out for Injuns, Mr Deacon. We got renegade Apaches roaming all over.'

'Don't listen to him!' snapped Mrs Peacock. 'Just a few half-starved youngsters, hiding up in the mountains and skulking out now and then at night to snatch a few head of beef. They ain't going to be bothering you!'

Vinny hadn't finished, 'And how about the devil riders?'

'Those evil men are only interested in robbing banks, and tearing the heart outa towns,' his mother said. 'They'll be fine, Vinny Peacock. Just you stop putting fretful notions in their heads. If two young folk can't take a ride out now and then, we may's well all go back east and live in some cramped closet in a city!' And riding through this lush cattle-country, with the grass swinging in the gentle breeze, that seemed like a poor prospect to Henry.

There was rougher terrain ahead, though, for sure, where the grazing was more ragged. Up there the trail started to steeple into that distant crowding landscape of chimney rocks and rearing jag-edged boulders bigger than cathedrals. He'd heard that it was a landscape shaped in a long-ago time when the world had boiled over like a vast cauldron, spewing liquid basalt and limestone in an unending stream.

The town of Diamond Rock, where Hiram Gliss ruled, was in there somewhere, he supposed, perched on the edge of the looming loneliness of the conifer specked higher peaks. In those ageless ravines, and deep-cut secret canyons a man might find his dream of riches, or maybe just find himself a stony grave.

He shook his head at all those fancy, poetic notions, and glanced at the woman beside him. 'I guess one of us has got to open their mouth. May as well be me.'

Mathilda's expression was coolly detached. She was wearing a plain calico shirt-blouse, sleeves rolled to her elbows, and open at the throat. Her slim neck was circled by a fine gold chain. Whatever she was wearing at the end of that was hidden under her blouse. One hand gripped the small rail at the edge of her seat, and the other flicked dust away from her tan-coloured skirt. 'I still don't know if there's much I can tell you. I'm not sure I should be here.'

He hauled on the lines a little to slow down the horses, who'd clearly decided that since he hadn't bothered them so far, they could set their own pace for this trip.

'Well you are here, and since we're not going back till we've called on Marty Wilson, you may as well make the best of it.'

'How much did they charge you for this rig?' she inquired suddenly.

Henry was taken off guard by the unexpected query, 'Why're you asking?'

'Tyres on all but one of the wheels are worn right through,' she told him briskly. 'Those traces have been mended so often that there's hardly an inch of original leather left in them. We'll be lucky to get much further before something snaps.'

'How about the horses, then?' he asked,

disgruntled. 'Want to climb down check their teeth?'

'The mare's fine. But the back on the gelding is a touch too sagged for my liking.' She grinned suddenly, and her face lit up with a gentle mockery. 'The livery owner rubbed his hands when he saw you coming, I'd say.'

'Wasn't much of a place,' he said, a little sourly. 'But it's the only one in the town. Didn't have much choice in the matter. Anyhow …' He frowned, 'How come you're so much of an expert on rigs and horseflesh?'

'My father ran a livery.'

'In Kansas?'

She turned her face from him abruptly. 'You were going to do the talking.'

'I guess I was.' He gave a half smile to himself. Well, he knew just a yard or two more about her than he had a few minutes ago. And if he'd known that this morning, he would have taken her down with him to collect this rig. Still, they were saddled with it now, for good or ill; no sense in wasting time worrying about whether it'd finish the jouney in one piece.

He took a breath. 'Last night I had a talk with the woman who lives with the judge.'

Mathilda nodded. 'I know you did. Saw you go up the hill. Saw you go inside the house.'

'Guess you are a spy then, at that!' he snapped, disconcerted. 'Then you also know I was only in there a few minutes.'

'Doesn't matter to me where you go at night,' Mathilda said stiffly. 'Though Mrs Peacock's told me about Juliet Young. Seems she snared plenty with her tight dresses, and come-hither eyes before Blackitt decided to give her house-room.'

'Yeah, well, she didn't snare me. And she told me something real interesting. Seems that Lew called on the judge on the morning of the day he got himself arrested for gunning down Stretch Finnegan.'

'You didn't know that?' Now she was looking at him hard. 'Blackitt never … mentioned it?'

'Blackitt claimed he'd never met Lew till he saw him standing trial.' He tugged the lines again, impatiently, 'You just slow yourself, mister!'

Mathilda laughed as one of the lines snapped, and with an oath he fought to keep his balance. 'Told you that'd happen.'

'So you did.' He heaved hard on the remaining lines and the horses came to a stop. 'You got a needle and thread on you?'

'It doesn't need that.' They both swung down, and he walked round to watch her deftly bringing together the broken leather. She spat on both ends, working them between her hands, and drew them together in a tight knot. She rubbed her hands on her skirt.

'That'll hold?'

'Should do.' There was a sparkle in those eyes that he hadn't seen much in the short time since they'd met; she'd enjoyed that little demonstration of her skill.

'Well, thanks, Mathilda. Lucky you decided to come along. Guess we can get moving again.'

'Just give me a minute.' She began to walk away.

'Where you going?'

Turning, she gave him a pitying little smile. 'Where do you think I'm going? You just keep your eyes turned well away from that clump of scrub oak, you hear.'

He grinned, and climbed aboard, but did give one little sideways glance, his eyes following the rocking sway of her hips under the skirt, as she headed through the long grass towards the twisted clump. Then he faced forward, Juliet Young, the judge's dark-eyed mistress, had doubtless snared a sizeable number of men in her time, but she had to work at it. Mathilda sent a shiver through him without even trying.

He sat there lost in his own thoughts for a minute of so, and then his flesh went cold as he heard her let out a terrified scream. He whirled round, and slammed down from his seat as he saw her running wildly from the clump of oak. She was gripping her left arm.

'What the hell is it?' he shouted.

'I think I've been bitten. A rattlesnake, maybe. I felt this pain in my arm just as I was standing up.' She was shaking with fear. 'Henry, do you know what to do?'

'Let me take a look.' Trying to keep a cool head, he gently prised her right hand away from her arm, just above the wrist. There certainly was a blotchy red mark there. All he could think was that he'd have to suck out the poison, and make damn sure he didn't swallow it.

Then, as he took a closer look, he threw back his head, letting out a relieved laugh. 'You see the snake, did you?'

'No, I just hauled up my … I just came running.' Her fear was abating. 'Not a snake?'

He ran a finger along that red mark, and then drew out a thorn, so small you could hardly see it. 'Wild gorse, I guess.' He flicked the barb away. 'You must've caught your arm against the bush.

Lucky it wasn't somewhere more ... tender!'

Mathilda stomped back to the buggy, and he fought off the urge to laugh again, as he rejoined her. 'Listen. I'm sorry I laughed. But you got to admit, we're a fine pair to be out here. A feller who used to work for his father's shipping company and a woman whose pa ran a livery.'

Her face was stony. 'Well, there's a touch more to me than that, Henry Deacon.'

'So you say. Though, as my old pal Chet Stookey would say, there's no fruit in a pudding till you've tasted it!'

'What does that mean?'

'It means that I don't rightly know if you are what you say you are, Mathilda.'

'Well, take a look at this then.' One hand fastened on the chain round her neck, and she drew it up slowly, and he saw that there was a US Marshal's shield attached to the end of it.

He cupped it in his hand; it was still warm from where it had been nestling against her body. 'You've been sworn in and everything?'

Taking it back, she let it fall back inside her blouse. 'I have. Sam insisted that I take the oath.'

'This'd be Sam McWheel, the feller you mentioned before?'

Mathilda nodded. 'It's a long story, Henry. I guess you have a right to know.'

'I'll drive this rig,' he said slowly, 'and you just talk, Mathilda. Though maybe you could tell me your real name before we start.'

'My real first name is Mathilda. Sam reckoned it'd make things easier for me.'

'Did he?' The rig bounced into motion, and Henry gave a low whistle. 'But not Mathilda

Farnell?'

'No. I was born Mathilda Collier. In Dove Creek, Nebraska.'

She told him how her father had owned a livery stable. Times were hard, and he'd borrowed heavily from a local loan-shark. 'We kept paying, but there was always so much interest owing. Like climbing a mountain that grew bigger every time you looked up.'

Eventually the loan-shark lost patience with a couple of delayed payments, and sent someone round to turn the screws a touch tighter. 'If ever a man was wicked, that one was. Wes Willis. Dressed all in black. The colour of his heart!'

Mathilda's face darkened, 'Made all kind of threats. Said he'd be back in a week, and if the money wasn't there, then … I wanted us to get out there and then. But Father was too darned stubborn. Said that something would turn up.' She shivered. 'All that turned up the next week was Wes Willis and two other men.'

It took her a little while for her to get herself to unravel the next strand in the tale. 'They were back a day earlier than they'd said. I wasn't there. Gone into Dove Creek to do some shopping.'

Her eyes were closed, and her face was deathly white. 'I arrived back to find they'd taken what few horses we had left. The buildings were burning, and my poor, poor father was lying in a lake of his own blood not able to move, just watching it happen. I thought we must have been raided by Indians.'

Henry swallowed hard at the picture she was painting. 'He managed to tell you what had happened?'

'Mostly,' she said in a low voice. 'Though he probably spared me the worst of it. They tied him down and tortured him. Said he must have some cash stowed somewhere ...'

She took a long breath. 'He died the next day. Willis and the others were long gone. Seemed he was wanted in a dozen states for murder, rape ... anything you care to name, he'd done it. And laughed as he did it!'

'It's a hell of a thing,' he muttered, not sure what else he could say.

'That was just over a year ago, now. I went east to stay with my aunt in Maryland. Quiet little place. Started to think I might settle down there.'

'Get married, raise a family?'

'I had an offer or two.' She managed a fleeting smile. 'Nothing I wanted to take up. Then Sam McWheel turned up at my aunt's house. An old friend of my father's from way back. I'd found an address for him in Washington when I was clearing out what was left of our belongings. Wrote him; told him what had happened to Father, and where I was going.'

They halted for a while then to rest the horses. Henry managed to get a fire going quick enough, and they boiled some water for coffee, and made a dent in the bread and baked ham Mrs Peacock had forced on them.

Mathilda painted a real vivid word picture of Sam McWheel; tall, gaunt and grizzled, a face burned by wind and weather until it looked like it had been carved from a chunk of old saddle leather.

'He'd visited us now and then in Dove Creek. I used to think he was something real special. A real frontier-man, done a lot of scouting for the army, fought Indians ...'

Sitting leaning against a wheel, she sipped her coffee, and laughed affectionately, 'Father knew he'd been working in some kind of secret job for a while. Government business. Hardly a place on the frontier that Sam hadn't ended up one time or another.'

Henry teased a sliver of ham from a front tooth. 'Including these parts?' he asked speculatively.

Mathilda tossed away the coffee dregs, and stood up. 'We'd better move on, Henry.'

'Sure.' He kicked dirt over the few remaining embers of the fire, making sure it was good and dead, and watched her climbing back aboard the buggy. He felt envious of Sam McWheel; she'd talked real fondly about that one. He'd be a hard man to compete with.

They headed on; the going got slower, as the terrain became more broken; over to the north he saw what he took to be cattle grazing, and even thought he saw riders moving round them. Mrs Peacock had told him Judge Blackitt owned a spread out this way; could be those men were working for him. But they were many miles off, Blackitt was even further away, and for all it mattered, he and this woman might be the only people in the world.

He listened while she told him about the man Sam called the Old Man, who could walk in on the President whenever he felt the need. 'He'd sent Sam down here when the Arizona Devils started becoming something more than just a nuisance.'

She pointed towards the mountains. 'He kitted himself out as a prospector. Took himself out to

Diamond Rock. Hiram Gliss has been around a long time. A thorn in the Old Man's side, you might say. He and Sam figured that if these devil riders had some kind of mountain hideout, then they'd more than likely choose a place within spitting distance of that town.'

Henry kept his eyes on the terrain ahead. He'd seen a wisp of wood-smoke a moment or two back, and now he could see the shadowy shapes of a couple of buildings. That'd be the Wilsons' place, he reckoned.

'And did Mr McWheel come up with anything in Diamond Rock?'

Mathilda nodded. 'He was sitting in the saloon one morning, when three riders came into town. Big men, big horses. Tied up outside Gliss's house. Didn't stay long, but Sam got a good look at them, and their mounts. One of them was riding a big black with a star-burst blaze on its head. The same horse had been spotted more than once when the devil riders galloped into some small town!'

Henry stared. 'So he found them? Then why …?'

'Why not send in a posse?'

'I guess that's what I was going to say,' he admitted.

'Wouldn't do any good,' she said. 'They need to be caught out in the open. On their way to cause misery to some other town.'

'Maybe.'

She shifted her position on the seat. 'We're almost there, aren't we?'

'The end of your story, or Marty Wilson's place?'

'Both,' she replied. 'Sam came back to Washington to chew things over with the Old Man. Seemed to them both that getting close to Gliss'd be a way of getting closer to the Arizona Devils. The Old Man's been hoarding information about Gliss and his doings for a long time.'

'Stuff that might turn out to be ... useful one day?' asked Henry.

'I guess so,' nodded Mathilda. 'Anyhow, he sent Sam down to Phoenix, to talk with someone else who might be glad to get Gliss off his shoulders.'

'This'd be your so-called uncle?'

She glanced at him, and he saw a flicker of admiration in those grey eyes. 'You've got a quick brain, Henry. Quicker than I thought when I first met you!'

He winced at the back-handed compliment, but let her carry on. 'His name's Mike Farnell. Somehow, the Old Man had found out that he owed Gliss a sizeable amount of money. It turned out his brother in Kansas had just died in a cholera epidemic. His niece, too.'

Henry nodded. 'And that gave Sam McWheel the idea?'

'That's it. Sam got Farnell to wire Gliss with the proposition of using his orphaned niece to pay off what was owing. He knew it was the kind of wicked bargain that'd suit Gliss.'

'And all Sam had to do was to find a girl willing to marry that skunk, so she could keep an eye on things in Diamond Rock!' Henry had been stunned by the audacity of what she'd been telling him. Now he shook his head in disbelief, 'And what in hell could you do if you did find out anything about the devil riders, Mathilda?'

'I'd pass it on to Sam. He's back in Diamond Rock right now,' she told him. 'Waiting for me to get there. And doubtless wondering where the hell

I am!'

'But what I don't understand, Mathilda, is why you'd agree to this. Sure, this McWheel guy's an old family friend ...'

She gave him a long look. 'One thing I missed out, Henry. Sam recognised the horse, sure. But he'd also seen the rider before.'

'Wes Willis?' he blurted out. 'Is that why you're doing this, Mathilda? Revenge for your father?'

Her face hardened. 'Maybe I was having doubts, after I met Gliss. But when I heard about those women who were gunned down in Benson yesterday, I knew I had to go on with it. Willis and his black-hearted pals are going to swing at the end of a rope. And I want to be the one who loops the noose round their evil necks!'

'But suppose Willis recognises you?'

'He never saw me,' she said. 'First time he came visiting I stayed in another room. I'd know him all right though. Next time, as I said, I wasn't there.'

They'd made a lot of ground while they'd been talking, and the cabin, and a large barn next to it were clearly in sight now. No sign of any movement there though, although there was still a feathering of wood-smoke coming from the cabin chimney. A few horses grazed placidly in the corral by the barn.

Henry's head was buzzing. 'So if Gliss is in on what this gang is doing, then maybe Judge Blackitt is too? And maybe my brother did find out something ...' He broke off, looking at her, questioningly.

'That's why I'm here with you,' she returned. 'I don't want Sam to think I've wasted my time.'

'I still reckon it's a crazy plan that he's cooked

up,' Henry commented, swinging the horses away from the main track onto the trail cutting down towards Marty Wilson's place. 'And I still hope you don't have to go through with marrying Gliss. Maybe something'll turn up.'

Mathilda gave a bitter laugh. 'Sure, just like it turned up for my father.' She looked towards the cabin. 'You reckon that the Wilsons are asleep?'

'Life can't be too hard if they've got time to do that,' he said. He pulled the horses to a stop a yard or so away from the cabin. 'Hallo there! Anybody home!'

Mathilda climbed down stiffly. 'Next time you hire a buggy, check the springs first. I'm aching all over.'

'Well, you go wake Marty and Shirley-May, and I'll get this team unhitched.'

'You can do that by yourself?' A little glint of friendly mockery showed in her eyes.

'I guess I can.' He glanced over towards the corral, and then he froze. Aware that Marty Wilson went in for rearing horses, he'd taken the beasts in the corral for granted, but now his eyes narrowed. Sure, there was a couple of young, unbroken colts, but the rest of them were too big-boned. They were saddle horses, and as one of them lifted its head from the thin grazing he saw the star-burst blaze glowing out of its dark head.

'Mathilda!' he yelled, 'Don't go near the ...'

Alarmed, she twisted round, but the door had already been yanked open, and two burly figures appeared. She screamed as one of the men grabbed her, and Henry desperately tried to lash the team horses into motion. But as Mathilda kicked and struggled in the doorway, there were more men coming through the door, side-arms in hand, and dashing towards the buggy.

Henry made a despairing move for his own gun, but then he found himself looking into the muzzle of a long-nosed Frontier Colt. 'Just you climb down real gentle, mister.'

The gunman stepped back. He was clothed in black; riding boots, levis, shirt and kerchief. The wide-brimmed hat was sloping back slightly atop a head of long, thick black hair. As a pair of chill, pitiless blue eyes surveyed him from under hooded lids, Henry knew with a terrible certainty that this was Wes Willis.

SEVEN

Dan Finnegan's pale, half-starved face broke into a grin of sardonic glee, as Willis propelled Henry roughly into the main living room of the cabin. 'Well, lookee here! The fastest city slicker in the West!'

Henry was in no state to think up a quick-fire answer, and just grunted something incoherent. It seemed that the devil riders didn't spend all their time holed up in the mountains, then, since he'd come across this one in Charity. Stretch Finnegan's son was standing behind a long settle on which Marty Wilson sat with his young wife. She'd clearly been crying, but she was pale and composed in a kind of fearful resignation now.

'You keep your itchy fingers off your gun, Finnegan,' ordered Willis testily. 'And you, Deacon, you set down with these fine folks you come visiting!'

Wincing at the brutal jab in his back, Henry twisted round, and sat down next to Marty Wilson's wife. She'd not long since washed her chestnut hair, whch was fluffy and tousled, held by a ribbon at the nape of her neck. She smelled of scented soap, but also of fear.

Mathilda had been slammed into a wicker chair

over in the corner. A swarthy, unshaven individual with a pencil-thin cigar hanging out of his mouth kept his frog-like eyes close on her. Her face was expressionless, but Henry saw her eyes confirming that the man in black was the one who had tormented and tortured her father.

If these men really were the gang that had been terrorising this part of the South-West then only a fool could think that he was going to come out of this alive. There were just two ways he could play it now, he supposed. He could act all humble, start begging pointlessly for his life. Or he could go down shouting.

'So how come you boys were waiting for me?' he inquired, as casual as if he was ordering a drink at a bar counter.

Willis flicked the side of his hawkish nose. 'Did I ask you to speak, mister?'

'No, you didn't,' Henry agreed. 'But you must want to do some talking else I guess I'd be dead already.'

Next to him, Shirley-May Wilson gave a frightened shake of her head. 'Don't ride them mister, whoever you are. These are the Arizona …'

From behind her, Dan Finnegan gave a harsh laugh, 'Devils. Arizona Devils. A real mean kinda name, hey Wes? We're just normal, everyday folks.'

Willis glowered. 'Never asked you say nothing, neither, Finnegan. You just get yourself outside and help with saddling the horses. We ain't staying much longer.'

'The others can manage without me, fine,' said Finnegan cockily. 'I don't wanna miss the fun in here.'

'If you're still in here in five seconds, boy,'

growled Willis, 'Then you're gonna miss the rest of your miserable life. Just git, when I say!'

Finnegan didn't argue this time. He scuttled out, past the bulky man standing by the door. His face was as impassive as a brick-built wall, and he held a snub-ended scatter gun by his side.

'Judge Blackitt let you know I was headed this way, did he?' asked Henry, leaning back. 'Daresay there's nothing much in Charity he doesn't know about.'

Marty Wilson said shakily. 'You're Lewis Deacon's brother? That's it, ain't it? You came out here to see if I could tell anything. Hell, you was wasting your time, mister. There's nothing to tell.'

Shirley-May let out a sob. 'And now we're all going to die!'

Mathilda provided a sudden diversion by letting out an aggrieved shriek. 'Get your hands off me!'

She shrank away as the swarthy man ran his fingers over her hair. His hand slid down onto her neck, inside the collar of her blouse. 'A real pretty chain you got there. Gold, I'd say.'

An instinctive revulsion at his touch shot her to her feet, and her eyes flashed. 'Just leave me be, will you!'

Casually, as if he was swatting a fly, he slapped her full handed across the face; the marks of his fingers livid against her skin. Mathilda staggered but stayed upright. 'Now you sit down, missie!' he snarled, 'And keep quiet. I want your chain, I'll have it, and anything else I care to take from you. Ain't that right, Wes?'

Alarmed by the idea that the marshal's shield might be brought into view, and anxious to try protecting Mathilda for as long as possible, Henry had started to rise from where he was sitting. The big man by the door swung up the scatter gun, and the barrels loomed as deep and as wide as twin railroad tunnels. 'You got a yearning for a harp and halo, boy, you just keep on moving.'

'That's enough,' barked Willis impatiently. He glared at Mathilda. 'You get back in that chair, and stay put. And Coffery, keep your goddamned paws to yourself for a couple of minutes.'

'Sure, Wes.' But Coffery's bulging eyes gleamed out of his dark face, and he hovered there like a hungry vulture over Mathilda, who slumped back hopelessly in the wicker chair.

Willis swivelled back to look at Henry. 'So, who sent you, Deacon? Who sent you here?'

Henry shrugged. 'Nobody sent me here. My brother was killed. Framed. Way I see it now, maybe he got some idea where you were hiding up. Thought he should tell somebody. Trouble was he went to tell Judge Blackitt.' He shook his head, 'Bad mistake.'

Willis had his gun in his hand now. 'You came all this way just to try clearing your brother's name?'

'Might sound strange to you,' returned Henry, 'But that's how it was. That's how it is.'

'Well, let's see,' said Willis thoughtfully. Without warning he yanked Henry to his feet, jamming the muzzle of his gun into Henry's neck, under the chin. 'I gave Finnegan five seconds to do like he was told, I'm giving you two to start telling me the truth!'

Willis's breath was unpleasantly hot on his face, smelling of tobacco, liquor and onions. 'Then you may as well shoot now. I can't tell you anything else!'

'How about telling me who's paying you?'

The gun-barrel was getting dangerously close to splitting Henry's windpipe, and he tried to stay statue-still. 'Paying me?' he croaked. 'Nobody's paying me.'

'Wouldn't be some leather-arsed US government monkey up in Washington, would it?'

Henry's brain cleared a little. So that was who they thought he was. From what Mathilda had told him about the Old Man's methods, he doubted they knew anything for sure. But all strangers were dangerous in their evil minds. Another time, another place maybe he would have laughed. A coward, he supposed, might have pointed a quaking finger at the grey-eyed girl in the wicker chair: 'Hell you got the wrong person, Willis. She's the one you want!'

He just stayed where he was though, feeling the seconds on his personal time-piece ticking away inexorably. Then all of a sudden Willis jerked the gun back and shoved Henry away. 'Ah, sit down. Maybe you don't set much store by your own gizzard. Could be there's a better way to get you singing.'

He reholstered his weapon. 'Seems like your time's come, Coffery.'

'What's that, Wes?'

'Just do whatever gives you pleasure with that woman there.' Willis shrugged indifferently. 'May as well use her, she ain't gonna be round much longer.'

Henry got his breath back. His blood ran cold. 'I'm telling you, Willis. I can't tell you any more than I've told you.'

'See, won't we?' retorted the gang leader

laconically. 'Coffery found out a long way back that there are easier ways of having fun with a woman than asking her first!' He chuckled crudely, 'And he sure loves having an audience!'

'Keep away from me, you animal!' Henry's heart was stabbed by a sharp, chill desperation as Coffery grabbed a handful of Mathilda's blouse, heaving her to her feet, and getting her in a kind of bear hug. It didn't matter what he did, what he said now.

Maybe he could claim to be a government agent; buy a little time that way, though it might be a painful time for him. He knew enough about the Old Man, about Sam McWheel too, to sound convincing. But something told him that Mathilda wouldn't want that. It was hopeless: Mathilda was staring humiliation and degradation in the face; and they were all standing with their toes over the edge of a deep-dug grave.

'You sure smell sweet girl!'

'You're just not human, Willis, letting him behave like that!'

Willis fired a contemptuous glance at Henry. 'You'd do the same, given half a chance, mister. Maybe you have already!'

Coffery held Mathilda tight, 'Come on, one little kiss, then we'll get down to the real business ...'

At that instant, a beam of light seemed to shine through Henry's whirling thoughts, and he yelled out, 'Maybe Hiram Gliss wouldn't be too happy about you damaging his property!'

Willis blinked, 'What in hell you talking about? What's Hiram Gliss gotta do with ...?'

At the same moment Coffery let out a pained yelp, and sprang away from Mathilda as if he'd been slapped on the haunch with a hot iron. There was blood surging from a deep bite on his left cheek. A blistering oath crackled through the air, and he sliced his hand down to pull his gun, doubtless set on pistol-whipping her into submission, but his fingers closed on empty air.

'She's got your gun, Coffery!' bellowed the man by the door. 'Get outa the way!'

Both barrels of the scatter gun spewed flame and smoke, and it was Coffery's ill-fortune that he'd moved angrily right in front of where Mathilda stood holding the revolver she'd snatched from his holster. The blast smashed him full in the side of the face, and he cannoned bloodily sideways, crashing into Mathilda and toppling on top of her.

In the same moment, as the bitter reek of gun-smoke swirled around them, the door was wrenched open. Henry heard Dan Finnegan yell out something. 'Wes. We gotta get outa here! The cavalry's coming!'

Willis whirled on him. 'What?'

Finnegan was staring at where Coffery lay in the corner, with Mathilda, sobbing, trying to extricate herself. 'A patrol. Cavalry. Just half a mile away. And moving fast!'

Wes Willis hesitated, and stared at the three people sitting in a line on the settle. He raised his gun, his finger tightening inexorably on the trigger. He was aiming unerringly at Henry's head, his hand as steady as a Redwood. Those icy eyes flickered, and he lowered the Colt. 'Your time'll come, mister!'

Then he and the man who'd killed Coffery were gone, following Dan Finnegan out to the horses. The remaining gang members rode off at a wild gallop, and with a last effort Mathilda rolled Coffery away from her, and staggered to her feet. She was a gruesome sight, her face and clothes splattered with the dead hoodlum's blood and brains. Letting out a wild howl, she stumbled towards Henry, and fell into his arms, her whole body shaking with gasping, almost silent sobs.

How long he stood holding her like that, Henry couldn't tell, but there was a nervous cough from the doorway and he turned to see a young cavalry officer standing there, the blue of his uniform muted under a heavy coating of trail-dust.

'You folks in trouble?'

Henry let out a grim laugh. 'Hell no, we're merry as a marriage bell! Just been having ourselves a real fancy hoe-down.'

Shirley-May, whose face was streaked with tears disentangled herself from her husband, and moved over to Mathilda. Hoarsely, she said, 'You come with me, and I'll help you get cleaned up.' Mathilda eased herself away from Henry, and followed the other woman through a door leading off the main room.

The cavalry officer edged inside, followed by a burly sergeant, with an impressive set of side-whiskers. 'I'm Lieutenant March, and this is Sergeant Danvers. What in Sam Hill's been going on in here?'

The sergeant walked over to where Coffery's body lay huddled, and stooped down to investigate. 'Scatter gun, I'd say. Makes quite a mess.'

'You'd be right,' said Henry. 'Shot by one of his own kind. Gentlemen, you just missed meeting the Arizona Devils.'

Lieutenant March paled. 'Those men we saw

riding off were the ...' He glanced at the sergeant, 'Maybe we'd better head on after them, sergeant.'

'Never catch 'em, sir. The horses need resting up now, anyhow. And the men, too.' He eyed Henry and Marty, 'We rode out from Fort Bowie couple of nights back. Been following the trail of a bunch of Apaches.'

The young officer glanced at him, clearly torn between the desire for the kind of glory which might come from catching the scourge of Arizona, and the need to keep good relations with his sergeant. 'I guess you're right, sergeant,' he said reluctantly. 'Tell the men we'll be staying for a while.'

The NCO turned smartly, and went back outside, and they heard him barking orders. Marty Wilson sank back onto the settle. 'If you soldier boys hadn't come by, I guess we'd be dead right now.'

'You're sure it was them? The devil riders rob banks, don't they?'

'They were waiting for me, lieutenant,' said Henry.

'And just why'd they be doing that, mister?' inquired March uncertainly. 'Just who are you?'

Henry's legs suddenly felt weak, and he sat down sharply next to Marty. 'Right now, it just doesn't seem to matter who I am. Only thing that matters is that I'm alive!'

Shirley-May refused to spend another night at the homestead until the Arizona Devils had been rooted out: 'They'll come back and next time we won't be so lucky. I am going back to Charity!'

Lieutenant March had declared roundly that

there was no possible way that the US cavalry could provide an escort for them. There was, he intoned, with the authority of a man who had digested every last syllable of regimental orders, no way he could authorise it. After a brief consultation with Sergeant Danvers, regimental orders had miraculously turned out to be a touch more flexible on such matters.

By the time they crested a low rise, and came in view of the glimmering lights of Charity, the moon was rising in a darkening sky. Far behind them the mountain peaks were etched against the deep blue sky, like giant black molars. Marty Wilson had shared the buggy with Henry, while the two women rode a small wagon just to the rear of them.

The cavalry detachment was now riding thirty or forty yards ahead. The soldiers were mostly young and bored with life in the remote outpost of Fort Bowie. And there wasn't too much excitement involved in their forays out to chase shadowy groups of Apaches venturing out to do a little cattle-stealing for the benefit of crooked Mexican ranchers across the border. So they'd seen the presence of Mathilda and Shirley-May as a real bonus, and earlier on there'd usually be half a dozen of them riding with the wagon, chatting animatedly to the two women and keeping their spirits up.

As they approached Charity, Marty was becoming gloomy again about leaving his stock behind. 'I guess they won't be there when I get back. If the Indians don't take them, then those fellers we crossed today'll be back to take them outa spite.'

'I guess it's partly my fault, Marty.'

The other man shrugged. 'Like I said before, Henry, it don't matter a whole lot. Some ideas are good, some are 'bout as solid as a rotted oak. Now if that trail up into the mountains through Diamond Rock had become a reg'lar stage route it might of been different.'

'You'd have been well placed to be a Way Station, you mean?'

Marty nodded. 'Who else? Thing is, though, the pass further north is easier going. And who in hell with any sense'd want to travel to Diamond Rock? Prospectors don't travel by stagecoach, and anyhow there's a lot less of them than there used to be.'

'Why's that?'

Marty shrugged. 'Hiram Gliss; he's got things sewed up tighter'n a whore's corsets. Try staking a claim in those parts, and he's likely to muscle in.'

He managed a grin. 'So, don't go blaming yourself that you wrecked things for me. Shirley-May's been griping on for weeks that we should go back and live with her ma! This has given her the excuse she was looking for.'

Henry laughed, 'A damn good excuse!'

'Oh sure it is.' He yawned, 'Still hard to figure how we're still alive, Henry. The man in the sky must of been looking our way at that minute.'

'And some,' breathed Henry with feeling. 'So, Marty, what'll you do? Go back to being a deputy?'

Rolling himself a smoke, Marty shook his head, as they began the downward incline into town. 'No, I've done with that. Long as Teale Ronson's the sheriff, anyhow. Locking up drunks so Blackitt can fine them ain't my idea of law enforcement. I'll find something to pay me enough to rent us a place so we don't have to live with Shirley-May's ma.'

Henry laughed. 'That idea doesn't appeal?'

'Why do you think I got us moved so far outa town?' Marty snapped a lucifer into life with his thumbnail and lit his cigarette, 'Though, I guess she wasn't the only reason. After the business with your brother, I got the feeling that eyes were boring into my back. Mr Whiting never said it was me went to fetch him over to the lock-up, but Judge Blackitt must of had his own ideas.'

They'd talked plenty about that night as they'd set out back towards Charity. Marty had nothing new to offer Henry. He'd come back into town late, after calling on Shirley-May and her mother to talk about wedding plans. He'd found Lew Deacon in one of the cells, with the sheriff snoring away drunkenly in his office, and he'd decided something had to be done.

Now, he said, 'Blackitt was barn-burning mad when he found out your brother had got himself a defence lawyer. Mr Whiting said he just happened to be passing the lock-up, and wanted a word with the sheriff. Still, it didn't do your brother no good, when it came to it.'

'Yeah, but you tried, Marty. And I'm grateful for that. Mr Whiting didn't hold out much hope that you'd be able to tell me anything. I was just snatching at loose straws. I could've got you and your missus killed.'

Lieutenant March had cut away from the head of his detachment and was riding back towards them. Marty sucked on his smoke. 'It beat all seeing Dan Finnegan with those boys. Everyone always figured that the Arizona Devils were … faceless men, maybe. Men from no place.'

'You think Stretch, his pa, might've been in on

the gang, too?'

He knew Marty didn't know the answer any more than he did. Vinny Peacock had told him that Stretch worked for Blackitt, so it seemed plain that Dan Finnegan took his meal ticket from the same source. Add that together and it was likely that Luther Blackitt and the Arizona Devils were tucked up in the same bunk. Before he said too much about that, though, Henry knew he needed to talk to Mathilda.

Lieutenant March reached them, pulling round to ride by them. 'Well, we all got here in one piece, gentlemen.'

'We're real grateful for the escort, Mr March,' said Henry. "Specially the ladies.'

'The US cavalry has never been slow to protect decent citizens,' returned March pompously. 'Even though, it does mean we've probably lost the trail of those Indians. I'm going to bivouac the detachment a mile or so outside town. I need the men with sober heads tomorrow.'

'I guess we'll be safe enough for the last mile,' said Marty, flicking his spent cigarette away.

'I'll ride in tomorrow to make my report to the town sheriff,' said the officer, 'And wire my superiors in Fort Bowie. I imagine this'll go all the way to Washington.' He looked at them both, 'And you may have to answer some questions from Federal agents in a few days.'

Henry fought back the desire to tell the Lieutenant that he'd be talking to a Federal agent a touch sooner than that. 'Sure. We'll be glad to do that, hey Marty?'

'I guess,' agreed Marty reluctantly. 'Won't be no harder than the ear-blasting I'm going to get from

Shirley-May's ma when she finds out what her daughter's been through!'

The cavalry officer rode back to his men. Henry didn't envy them a night in the open within stone-throwing distance of all the pleasures Charity had to offer thirsty and lonely men. That was the army for you, though. He turned and called back to the wagon behind. 'Soon be home, ladies!'

He got no response, and he faced front again. One of the many things troubling him, was what he'd yelled out just before Coffery caught the full force of the scatter gun. When Gliss learned that his intended wife had been at the Wilsons' homestead he mightn't be too pleased.

That was on Mathilda's mind, too, as they walked back from the livery stable, after returning the rig. They were skirting the edge of town, keeping away from the clamour of Main Street. 'Gliss'll start to wonder what I was doing there. Could make things difficult.'

'You're in deep enough water already,' Henry commented. 'A few more inches won't make much difference. Anyhow, after today, maybe Gliss'll be lying low. Maybe you'll never see him again.'

'And what about Sam?' she asked, 'He's there in Diamond Rock. What happened today doesn't change much. We don't know much more than we did before. They're brutal, unfeeling, and they got away.'

'Blackitt must be behind it, though,' he cut in. 'That woman of his, Juliet. Could be she knows more than she said to me. Find the weakest part of a wall, and push hard on it, that's the way, isn't it?'

Mathilda slipped her arm though his. 'You make it sound very easy, Henry Deacon. I just wish it was

Wes Willis had got in the way of that scatter gun.'

'His time'll come,' he muttered.

'Just what he said to you,' she returned. 'There's so much evil in that man I half expected maggots to come wriggling out of his skin.'

They reached the back of the Wells Fargo depot, and cut across onto the road up the hill again. It seemed a long time since this morning. Mathilda rested her head on his shoulder a moment as they approached Mrs Peacock's house. 'I'm glad you're still alive, Henry.'

He grinned, 'I'd be sorry to lose you, too ...' He stopped, and turned to look down at her. She was dusty, she was tired, there was a bruise on her cheek where Coffery had hit her, but she looked so darned lovely.

As he started to bring his face closer to hers, the front door of Mrs Peacock's house was jerked open. 'Hold it right there, Deacon!'

Framed against the light of the hallway, he saw a short, squat figure and a larger, bulkier shadow behind him. Naturally there was a gun pointed straight at Henry.

'This is becoming tiresome,' growled Henry. 'I guess from that badge on your chest, you'll be the town sheriff.'

Teale Ronson was not a pretty sight. If you looked too close at his shirt you'd probably be able to make out what he'd had for supper for the last few days. His britches were held up by sagging braces, and he had a day's growth of bristle on his flabby chin. He started to say something, and then he was shoved to one side, and Luther Blackitt joined him.

'Not hard to figure which of you is in charge, is it?' said Henry.

'He tries to make a run for it, Ronson, you put a hole in his scrawny chest!' Blackitt boomed.

Mathilda stepped sharply in front of Henry. 'He'll have to shoot me first!'

An upstairs window opened, and Mrs Peacock thrust her head out. 'You harm either of my guests, Teale Ronson, and I'll hang you myself. Now you come unlock this door, and let me out.'

Henry eased Mathilda to one side. 'You can put your gun down, sheriff, I'm not running anywhere. What's all this about?'

It was Luther Blackitt who replied. 'Seems I was right about bad blood running in families, Deacon. Your brother was a murdering skunk, and you're just the same.'

'What're you talking about? I've killed nobody. I've been outa town since just after first light. And I've got witnesses. Including a whole platoon of US cavalry!'

He saw Blackitt's eyes narrow. The fat little sheriff shook his head, keeping the gun pointed, and resting his other hand on the star hanging from his stained vest. 'Don't matter where you been today, mister. Last night we're talking about.'

Blackitt took a step towards him, and waved a fist in his face. 'Up at my place, weren't you? Forcing yourself on little Juliet.'

'Little Juliet? I talked to her, that was all.'

'Just move outa the way, judge.' Ronson was making a fruitless attempt to sound aggressively efficient. 'Seems you figured that talking wasn't enough. We got a witness saw you go in there. You come out maybe an hour later.'

'I wasn't in there that long!' Henry protested.

Blackitt came for him again. 'She's dead, Deacon.

Juliet's dead. You forced yourself on her and she fought back, and you got your murdering hands round her pretty neck, and you choked her to death.'

'You can't be serious!' Mathilda shouted.

Sheriff Ronson waved the gun, and suddenly there was a rapid clicking sound over the far side of the street. Three men stepped out, each aiming a cocked Winchester.

'Just start walking, Deacon. You're spending tonight in the lock-up.'

Blackitt gave a grim, menacing laugh. 'Just like your brother did!'

EIGHT

'Don't you ever get this place cleaned up, Ronson?'

The door at the end of the narrow passage leading to the three cells was open, and Henry could see the sheriff lounging in his chair. Teale Ronson got to his feet, glowering at him. 'This ain't a hotel, Deacon. And I got a Mex woman comes in every few days.'

'It's the smell. Like you've been keeping a dozen hogs in here!'

Ronson slouched nearer to the cell door. 'Sour whisky breath clings, I guess. We get a lot of drunks spending the night in here.'

'So that Blackitt can line his pocket-book?'

'If they get drunk and cause a ruckus,' he snapped, 'Then they're breaking the law, and I'll arrest them.'

'Just like you arrested my brother?'

Ronson hesitated. 'Wasn't me arrested him. A citizens' posse brung him in. They seen what he done to Stretch Finnegan.'

Henry gave a hoarse laugh. 'Citizens' posse? What in hell's name is that? Another way of saying lynch mob?'

The sheriff hooked his stubby thumbs through his braces, and there was a defensive twitch in his bristling cheeks. 'He wasn't lynched.'

'You try to help him?' Henry jabbed a finger at the narrow cot behind him, draped with a filthy blanket. 'For hell's sake he couldn't have gotten more beat-up if he'd been mowed down by a railroad locomotive.'

'He was mussed up, sure,' Ronson backed away a little, as though afraid that Henry's ferocity would give him the strength to snap the bars with his bare hands. 'But he was breathing steady enough.'

Henry shook his head in contempt, 'So you just went back in your office, slouched back in your chair, tipped your hat over your scaly head and went off to sleep.'

'I never did.' But he faltered, 'Who told you that?'

'Just a guess,' grunted Henry. He realised he'd learned that fact from Marty Wilson, and should keep it to himself. 'Anyhow, you weren't exactly wide awake when Mr Whiting called by.'

Suddenly, he got the distinct feeling that Ronson was wavering under his stare. Maybe the man was just a hog-fat slob who let Blackitt kick him whichever way he chose. Or maybe there was a glimmer of conscience flickering away inside his head. 'Just who were these concerned citizens who brought Lew in here?'

The sheriff came closer to the bars again. Perspiration beaded his slimy skin with a fine dew. There was an unpleasant whine in his voice. 'This ain't much of a job, mister. Maybe I ain't much of a lawman. But Stretch Finnegan was dead. Even here folk kinda frown on shooting a man from behind. Maybe they did slam into your brother a touch too hard, but he was guilty wasn't he?'

'No, he was not. But even if he was guilty as hell, would that makes it right?' retorted Henry.

'I keep my head down,' Ronson said dully. 'Listen, if I could get outa here I would. But I'm just too damned old, mister. I lose this job, I'll end up shovelling horse-shit in a livery stables, or something.'

'Might be a better job than you got here!' Henry turned away, and went back to the bunk against the wall.

The sheriff stayed where he was. 'Wasn't always like this, you know.' He stabbed a finger at his chest. 'Me, I've eaten a trail-herd's dust and raised myself a crop of blisters at round-up. Always rode point and you know how blamed dangerous that is. I was a good cowhand.'

'That so?'

'Managed to save enough to buy my own place,' said Ronson eagerly. 'Small ranch. Couple o' hundred head of stock. Something I could call my own.'

Slumped back morosely, Henry glowered. 'I don't recall asking to hear your life story, Ronson.'

The sheriff didn't seem to hear him. 'My wife got sick. And my two babbies. Smallpox. You know what that means, Deacon?'

'It means they died, I guess.'

Ronson had his hands gripped tight round the bars now. 'Sure they died. And maybe I died with 'em. 'Cept I carried on living too. Joe Rand bought my spread from me. Gave me a decent price and I drunk it away.'

All at once there was real feeling in his voice; an echo of the man he might have been once. 'Now you can look at me like I was a piece of stinking carrion, but I never killed no-one, and the way it looks you choked that judge's lady-friend to death! So you just tell me who's the better man outa me'n you.'

He jumped in panic as a hand clamped on his shoulder. 'Quite a speech, Teale. Never heard you string so many words together.'

Ronson let out a long, relieved breath. 'Didn't hear you come in, Mr Whiting. You want to see this one?'

Grover Whiting's bearded face looked in at Henry. 'Seems you've taken more care of him than you did of his brother. Not a mark on him as far as I can see.'

Henry pushed himself on to his feet. 'Just a few flea bites from whatever was wrapped in this blanket last night, that's all.' He stretched a hand through the bars. 'Glad to see you again, Mr Whiting. Guess Mrs Peacock and Mathilda did like I said, then.'

'They came calling on me, certainly. Maybe I can do a better job this time. Make up for what happened to your brother.' The lawyer swung round and glared at Teale Ronson. 'He's charged with murder? You got witnesses?'

'Someone seen him going in, and coming out of the judge's house.'

Whiting smiled coldly, 'And you're not going to tell me who that was?'

'You'll find out at the trial, Mr Whiting. That's how it's done.' Ronson heaved hard on his braces. 'Don't want witnesses being interfered with, do we?'

'No point in asking if you've got any other evidence, then?'

Ronson shook his head. 'We got enough proof he was the one strangled that woman. Take it from me.'

Whiting sighed, 'But I've got to wait till tomorrow. At the trial?' He didn't wait for an answer. 'Maybe you'd fetch me a chair so I can sit comfortable in there with my client.'

'I don't have to do that,' Ronson protested. 'You get your own chair, mister. I'll need to search you, too. Make sure you ain't carrying no gun.'

Whiting looked back at Henry. 'It wouldn't do you any good, if I did slip you a gun. 'Less you wanted to shoot yourself. If you managed to get your nose outside the place it'd be shot off. There's half a dozen armed men posted round the lock-up.'

'Hadn't planned on going anywhere,' said Henry.

The elderly lawyer waved at Ronson, 'Come on, get back in your office. I'll fetch a chair, you can search me, and then you can lock me in with Mr Deacon here.'

Ronson scuttled ahead of him back down the passageway. Whiting was soon back, carrying a small chair, and Ronson unlocked the cell door, swinging it open with a complaint of unoiled hinges.

'Now you get back in your office, Teale,' said Whiting as the sheriff re-locked the door. 'And you can shut that door at the end of the passage. Let me have a confidential talk to my client.'

'Spouting to you all he wants, won't make no difference.' Stalking off, Ronson slammed the door.

Whiting wrinkled his long nose, and twitched a hand at his pointed beard. He sat down on the rickety chair. 'Miss Farnell told me about what happened to you up at the Wilson place. You were damn lucky, I'd say.'

'She told you Dan Finnegan was one of them?'

'Can't say I'm surprised,' said Whiting. 'Makes you wonder how many other members of the Arizona Devils come wandering into Charity of an evening.'

'Calling on their boss, maybe,' suggested Henry. 'Because seems pretty clear to me that Luther Blackitt's behind them somewhere.'

'Now hold on,' the lawyer cut in sharply, 'This case isn't about the devil riders. It's about you, Henry, and the murder of Juliet Young. Don't start muddying the waters with wild accusations.'

'Wild, are they?' snapped Henry bitterly. 'Wes Willis and the others were waiting for me at Marty's place. If that doesn't have Blackitt's cross on it, I don't know what does. I get back here, and he's waiting to have me arrested for killing his lady-friend ...'

Whiting lit a small cigar, and puffed on it reflectively. 'And she'd told you that your brother had come visiting the judge that day.'

Henry leaned forward. 'It all starts adding up. We figure Lew rode back here from Skull Canyon, 'cause he'd come on the place where the devils were hiding up.'

'We?' queried Whiting thoughtfully.

Henry shrugged, 'I was talking about it with Mathilda. Anyhow, he goes to see Blackitt, who has him framed to get rid of him. Now I'm getting too close at the truth and Blackitt's doing the same to me. Makes sense doesn't it?'

'Why'd Judge Blackitt be getting this gang to

raise hell all over the territory, then?'

'Place suits him as it is,' returned Henry. 'That's all I can think. Keep decent folk from settling in the territory and he carries on with his lawless ways.'

Whiting rubbed his chin. 'Guess it's possible. But right now, we've got to think of how we get you off this charge. In a civilised town you wouldn't come to trial for weeks. Here, they wrap things up quick and neat.'

Henry nodded slowly. 'Daresay the outcome'd be the same tomorrow or next week. What chance do I stand at this trial with him presiding over things?'

Tapping away a cone of ash from his cigar, the lawyer pondered the problem, his eyes half-closed and Henry sensed he was none too cheerful about what the outcome might be. 'A whole lot depends on who they'd trawled in as a witness. Maybe I can shake his story.'

'If Blackitt lets you get on with it!'

Whiting studied him with grim sympathy. 'I could tell you how it's the jury decides, and not the judge. But you know the way things shape up here. Trouble is you did go into Blackitt's house, didn't you?'

'For a few minutes, that's all. The woman was drunk. We just talked. She was alive when I left.' Reaching out, Henry touched him on the shoulder. 'I guess you'll do your best, Mr Whiting. But I can't expect the cavalry to come riding to my rescue twice in two days.'

'Dammit,' Whiting snapped, 'Just get rid of this death-wish, Henry. There's always a chance.'

'I know,' muttered Henry. 'I'll bear that in mind, Mr Whiting. But I'd like you do something else for me, if you would. Won't help me, but might help someone else.'

He'd been thinking about it ever since he was flung into the stinking cell. Hiram Gliss might come back into town any time. If things tomorrow went as badly as he thought, then Mathilda would soon be on her way out to Diamond Rock. Sure, he'd be dead by then, wouldn't matter a spit in the wind to him. But it mattered now. Maybe she would carry off the play-acting, get in touch with Sam McWheel. Or maybe it'd all go wrong. Just thinking about what that bastard Coffery was planning for her still sent his blood cold as night. If she was out there, all alone, surrounded by unpitying enemies …

'I won't let it happen!' he burst out.

Whiting was just sitting, watching. 'Won't let what happen, Henry?'

'I want you to contact Washington, Mr Whiting.'

The lawyer blinked uncertainly. 'About your encounter with the Arizona Devils? That what you mean? I wasn't there, Henry, what can I tell them? I'm just a back-country lawyer.'

'Said you had ambition once,' Henry reminded him. 'Maybe this'd be a way you could get yourself noticed. Maybe if you do this you won't have to finish your days out here.'

'Do what, for God's sake?' exclaimed Whiting impatiently.

Henry took a deep breath, and stared towards the door at the end of the corridor. He lowered his voice. 'Thing is, Mathilda … she's not quite what she seems.' He shook his head, 'Hell, I shouldn't be telling you this, Mr Whiting. She'd kill me!' He let out a rasping laugh. 'That's a real clever thing to say. She won't have to, will she?'

'Fight's not over yet, Henry. Maybe the jury'll see it your way.'

'And maybe hogs'll sprout wings. No, Mr Whiting, I've got no choice. Mathilda she's out here on government business. She's, hell, she's a sworn in Federal marshal.'

Whiting raised a warning hand. 'Do I really need to hear this, Henry? Do I want to hear it?'

Henry forced a grin. 'You're my lawyer, Mr Whiting. You were the only friend Lew had in this town. Who else'm I going to tell? Teale Ronson, Luther Blackitt?' He knocked his hand against the solid wall of the lock-up. 'This wall? I want those office-bound fellers up in Washington to know they just can't leave her and Sam McWheel out here. They gotta find some other way of dealing with things.'

'Sam who?' Whiting ran a hand through his thinning hair. 'Henry, just slow down!'

A chorus of hooting and jeering trumpeted out as Teale Ronson, and three other armed men, accompanied Henry into the courthouse the following morning. Henry had spotted it the other day, set back from Main Street at the far end of town. A big barn of a place with a lot of fancy carving and plasterwork. He got the strong feeling that Luther Blackitt's hand was behind the construction of this outlandish addition to the skyline of Charity. It was like Blackitt's house, puffed to bursting with self-pride. Like the man himself.

Forty long pine benches filled the room and every inch of them was weighted to capacity. The citizenry of this township had plainly turned out in full force to watch the wheels of justice spin on their doubtful way.

The fact that the jury, lined up near where Blackitt sat behind a high table, joined in the generally unfriendly greeting did nothing to liven his spirits. He joined Grover Whiting at a table just below where Blackitt was sitting. One of the men who'd come in with him, shuffled to a seat behind him.

'One move, Deacon, and you're buzzard meat.'

Henry glanced at his lawyer. 'I'm buzzard meat whether I move or not, Mr Whiting.'

He turned round and looked at the faces behind him, half-expecting to see Mathilda and Mrs Peacock somewhere. But the only female faces, right at the back, belonged to some of the girls from the Paradise. They might add a touch of feminine colour to the scene, but they were just as raucous as the men in joining in the barrage of catcalls and hissing which began when he turned.

Judge Blackitt slammed his gavel down. 'Just cut the cackle. This here is a duly constituted court of Arizona Territory.' He glared down at the court clerk, hunched unhappily at another table. 'Get the charge read out, Mellick, and be quick about it!'

The scrawny man shuffled to his feet. 'He's charged with killing Mis' Young, judge. At your house, night before last. Strangled her till she was dead. Funeral's this afternoon. Three o'clock.'

Blackitt thumped his gavel again. 'Any witnesses?'

Mellick nodded. 'Sure, we got someone saw the whole thing, judge.'

Grover Whiting was suddenly on his feet. 'I don't see any prosecutor in this court, judge. How can a court be properly constituted without one?'

Blackitt stared down at him maliciously. 'I'm the

judge here, I say what goes. You just take care of defending your feller. If you can!' He raised his voice, 'Call the witness!'

Mellick shambled round, staring into the courtroom. 'You there, Joe Rand?'

Henry looked back again. A tall, rangy figure stood up near the back, and made his way up to the front. To Whiting, he muttered, 'He's a rancher, isn't he? Got a spread out to the west.'

Whiting nodded. 'An important man round here, Henry. And half the men on the jury work at his place, I'd say.'

Henry slumped back in his chair. 'Well, that's just about nailed the lid over me, hasn't it?'

Rand took his hat off. He was wearing a store bought suit for the occasion, but it didn't fit him, and it didn't suit him. He was a cattleman to his fingertips.

'You swear to tell the truth?' gabbled Mellick.

'Sure,' said Rand, and he took a glance at Henry. But his weather-lined face was impassive and Henry couldn't tell what he might be thinking.

Blackitt leaned forward. 'Good of you to come forward, Mr Rand. Just tell the jury what you seen the night before last.'

The rancher twisted his hat in his hands. 'Won't take much telling,' he said. 'I was visiting up on the hill near your house, judge. Upstairs window of the room where I was, it looks right across to your place. I saw Deacon come up the hill and saw him meet up with Mis' Young. Outside, close by that old oak you got there. Then they went in the house, and I saw the lamps being lit in a room at the front.'

'You got mighty good eyesight, Joe,' remarked Whiting, staying seated.

'You wait your turn,' Blackitt ordered. He looked at the jury, and mopped his face with his red bandanna. Then stuffing it back in his pocket, he tugged at his lapels. 'This is all kinda painful for me, fellers. But it's my duty to sit here and listen to it.'

Henry scowled at the pious tone, as he looked the judge up and down. There was something different about him. Then he realised what it was. Blackitt wasn't wearing that weightily expensive watch chain. His scowl deepened; it was a trivial kind of thing to be noticed by a man being shoved ever nearer the gallows steps.

The rancher was carrying on with his evidence. 'Anyhow, I saw them talking. Seemed to be having some kind of argument. Deacon was shaking Mis' Young.'

'Had his hands round her throat, did he?'

Rand hesitated for a moment. 'Guess he might of done, judge. Anyhow, I looked away for a while. I don't care to be a snoop, you understand.'

'Nobody thinks bad of you for looking, Mr Rand,' interjected the judge.

'Anyhow,' the rancher carried on, after a pause, 'Next time I looked, I seen Deacon heading off down the hill. Mis' Young was still inside, stretched out on a sofa or something. I figured she must be asleep. So I pulled the drapes. Never thought nothing more of it.'

He glanced round at Henry. 'But I guess she must of been dead. Only wish I'd gone after you then, mister.'

Unable to restrain himself, Henry sprang up. 'Hell, she wasn't dead when I left her. Sure, I had words with her. But when I cut out of there she was still alive!'

Blackitt hammered his gavel down thunderously. 'You calling Mr Rand a liar? Hell, boy, he's lived in these parts for thirty years. You been here a few days, and you don't exactly come well-recommended!'

The crowded courtroom throbbed with noise again, and Whiting hauled Henry back. 'Let me do the talking.'

He stood up once the clamour had died down. 'Mr Rand. Just who were you calling on that time of night? And why were you standing in an upstairs window?'

'That ain't none of your business.' The gavel sliced noisily a couple of times. 'This feller's sworn an oath to tell the truth, Whiting. Why he was up on the hill ain't rele … It ain't important!'

'But suppose somebody else came by later?' Whiting tried, fighting against the din growing behind him. 'If my client's telling the truth, and Miss Young was still alive when he left …'

'Well he ain't, and she wasn't!' declared Blackitt. 'Now if you got no witnesses yourself, Grover Whiting, I figure the jury can start reckoning up their verdict.'

'You hold on, Luther Blackitt!' The woman's voice came from the back of the courtroom, near the door. 'There's a witness here you ain't heard from!'

A hundred pairs of eyes stared at Mrs Peacock, who stood there with Mathilda. She was dressed in old-fashioned finery, with a bonnet which had seen better days. And she had a blistering air of purpose about her which silenced Blackitt as the two women came marching up past the lines of crowded benches.

Mrs Peacock stood below where Blackitt sat, and folded her arms: 'This one's got something to tell you, judge.' She glared at Mathilda, who stood dejectedly by her. Henry felt a sudden flare of hope. Mathilda was playing the destitute orphan again; next to her a frightened rabbit would have looked ferocious.

'You know about this, Henry?' asked Whiting out of the corner of his mouth. 'What're they playing at?'

Henry shook his head. Blackitt's voice boomed out. 'If you ladies is just wasting the court's time, then maybe you'll spend a few hours in the lock-up.'

Mathilda started to turn away, but Mrs Peacock grabbed her arm. 'You say what you gotta say, young lady. Never mind the shame of it. You jus' tell the truth.'

Every voice in the courtroom was stilled. Shame, Mrs Peacock had said. That was a good word. It looked like they were in for something fruity now, and nobody wanted to miss a thing. Even Judge Blackitt looked interested, if a touch uneasy.

Mathilda looked up at him. In a shaky voice, she said, 'Please, your honour. Mr Deacon couldn't have killed that lady up at your house.'

'We just heard Joe Rand say he saw it happen.'

Mathilda shook her head. 'I don't know what anybody saw. I only know what happened. I saw Mr Deacon go up the hill, and go in your house with ... with Miss Young.'

'We know that!'

'But I followed him, judge. I was kinda jealous.'

Blackitt glowered, 'Jealous? Hell, girl, you're promised to Hiram Gliss.'

'That's why I didn't want to say anything. I knew Mr Gliss'd be kind of, annoyed. But Mr Deacon had been real kind to me. I didn't want him getting in trouble with you, judge. So I slipped in the house, and told him to come out. Miss Young wasn't too pleased. And I swear she was alive when me and Henry … Mr Deacon went back to Mrs Peacock's house.'

Joe Rand cut in. 'I guess she could be telling the truth, judge. I didn't see her, but doesn't mean she wasn't there. And if Mis' Young was just sleeping…'

Mrs Peacock looked at him. 'Maybe we should call Polly Parker as a witness, Joe Rand. Ask what she saw.'

'I never said I was with Polly,' said the rancher flustered.

'Only place you could see the judge's house that clear. And sure as eggs you wouldn't be standing up all night in Polly's bedroom!'

'You hold your horses, Joe Rand,' yelled Blackitt, but it was plain that the jury were thinking hard about what Mathilda, and now Joe Rand had said. 'Doesn't mean Deacon didn't come back later.'

'He didn't!'

He stared down at Mathilda. 'Now how come you're so sure of that, missie?'

''Cause he spent the night in her bed!' Mrs Peacock had shouted the words out. 'I saw them go in her room. Mine's a respectable house, judge. Made me sick to the stomach to think of what those two unmarried folk were doing in there, it did. Couldn't sleep a wink all night.' She glared at Mathilda, 'And that bedroom door never opened till after first light!'

The audience cheered, and one or two of the jury waved their hats in the air. Mathilda just looked down at the floor, like she was wishing it would swallow her up. Whiting turned to Henry, keeping his voice low. 'They've cooked that up real nice between them, haven't they?'

The head juryman eased himself to his feet, and the noise subsided. 'Seems to me, judge,' he said confidently, 'That Mr Deacon here's got no case to answer. 'Cept to Mis' Peacock, that is!'

For the next minute or two, Blackitt nearly broke his gavel trying to hammer the wild audience into submission. At last he succeeded. 'I guess we'll have to dismiss the case!' he snarled. 'But if he didn't do it, then who did?' His eye fixed on Sheriff Ronson. 'Teale Ronson you come see me soon as you like. Someone killed little Juliet, and you gotta find out who!'

NINE

Grover Whiting folded the newspaper he'd been reading and laid it on his desk as the two newcomers came through his office door. 'I figured you'd be in to see me.'

Mathilda wasn't about to stand on ceremony. Planting herself in front of his desk, she folded her arms. 'Henry here has just told me that he's been letting his mouth run away with him, Mr Whiting. I swore him to secrecy, about my ... mission. And now he's blabbed it all to you.'

The old lawyer gave a faint smile at the girl's blistering tone. 'He was thinking of you, my dear lady. Remember, he reckoned he was half-way up the gallows steps when he told me about ... your little secret.' His grin twitched wider, 'He didn't know that you and Mrs Peacock were going to cook up that meaty tale giving him an alibi!'

Mathilda flushed, and her eyes fell on the newspaper. 'I can't imagine why you're reading that garbage, Mr Whiting!'

Vinny Peacock had hurried in at breakfast time with the latest edition of the *Charity Messenger*. 'Ink's hardly even dried on it,' he'd exclaimed. 'Mr Fletcher must of been up all night writing it and printing it.'

Whiting opened the paper out. 'Wilkes Fletcher has a vivid imagination, certainly,' he said wryly. 'Especially as I didn't even see him in the court yesterday.'

Henry shook his head. 'Mathilda didn't take kindly to being called a fallen woman.'

Whiting grinned, and read aloud. '*She wept as she saved her lover from a hang-rope by telling of their night of lust …*'

'Vinny's right!' snorted Henry. 'Only one good use for that particular publication!' He glanced at Mathilda, 'But he's right enough about you saving me from the noose.'

'And now Teale Ronson's got to set about finding the real killer,' mused Whiting. 'So I guess we'll never know who did it, and why.'

'That's not what I came to talk about!' snapped Mathilda, fiery again. 'I came to tell you to forget what Henry here told you about why I'm here. Just put it all to the back of your mind! I should never have got him involved, and it's surely not your concern.'

Henry had been trying to talk some sense into her all morning. He tried again. 'There's no way you can go out to Diamond Rock now, Mathilda. Hiram Gliss is as likely to have you strung up as to welcome you as his blushing bride. And what about Wes Willis and the Arizona Devils? You escaped them once. That kind of luck never holds, take it from me.'

She glowered. 'So I leave Sam out there to rot, do I? He trusted me enough to get me this job …'

'Hold on one moment.' Whiting cut in. 'If this boss of yours is as clever as you've told young Henry here, then I shouldn't worry too much, Miss …

Farnell.'

Mathilda looked at him suspiciously, 'My boss? Oh, sure he's clever. But until he gets told ...'

'He's been told!' said Whiting bluntly. 'Well, as much as I figured I could tell him in a wire. Didn't Henry here tell you that was the plan he'd come up with?'

'You sent the Old Man a wire?' At that moment Henry was relieved Mathilda wasn't toting a gun. The blazing light in her eyes was dangerous enough. She reached forward and grabbed the newspaper, 'Why not tell the editor of this rag-bag? He can let the whole town know!'

'Give me some credit, madam.' Whiting spoke with a crisp dignity. 'I was very circumspect in what I wrote. I have a copy somewhere.' He scrabbled round among the papers on his desk, but was unsuccessful in his search. He leaned back, tugging at his little beard. 'Well, it's here somewhere. But I assure you I worded it very carefully. This Old Man of yours will certainly get the gist of what's going on out here.'

'If the wire ever reaches him!' she snapped. 'Could just sit on a clerk's desk in Washington for days. Either way, I'm finished as a US marshal.'

Miserably, she sank into a chair. 'I've let everyone down. All because I thought I saw a way of getting revenge for what Willis did to my father.'

'Now hold on!' said Henry. 'You've let nobody down. It was a crazy notion in the first place. And I'm just glad that Hiram Gliss didn't ride off to Diamond Rock with you that first day!'

She wasn't going to be consoled, though. 'Right now those devil riders can carry on doing as they please.' Warningly, she waved Henry back. 'I don't need comforting, Henry Deacon.' Now she looked hopefully at Whiting, 'Do you reckon that your wire'll have some effect then? Maybe they might send some help out.'

The lawyer pondered the question. 'As I told Henry here, I worked up in Washington for a while. Nothing ever seemed to get done in a hurry. I guess you might have to sit tight for a few days.'

'Oh sure,' she muttered. 'A few days more for Wes Willis and his gang to terrorise some more small towns. More robbery. More murder of innocent folk. Just what's the point of it all, Mr Whiting?'

She didn't get an answer. Boot heels clattered in the hallway, and Teale Ronson appeared in the doorway, sweat beading his heavy face, and panting with a breathless urgency.

Whiting eyed him coldly. 'I'm busy, sheriff. Whatever it is, I daresay it can stay tied to the hitch-rail for a few more minutes.'

Ronson thrust past Henry, and fished in the pocket of his stained vest. Then he slammed something on the desk. 'I know who killed Miss Juliet, Mr Whiting.'

The lawyer picked up his eye-glasses and hooked them on, joining Henry and Mathilda in peering down at what Ronson had put on the desk.

'That's part of a chain, isn't it?' asked Henry.

'Sure is!' confirmed Ronson. 'Three links off of a watch-chain. Dub Wickett brung them to me.'

'Dub's the town undertaker,' cut in Whiting, picking up the chain links and examining them more closely. 'Where'd he get them, Ronson?'

The lawman hitched up his sagging britches. 'Outa Miss Juliet's hand. Said she'd been gripping 'em real tight. Had one helluva job prising them out of her fingers while he was fixing her up to be buried.'

Mathilda let out a cry. 'You mean she was grabbing them as she was ... choked to death?'

'Figure that's how it was,' muttered Ronson.

Whiting took off his glasses. 'And you have a notion where they might have come from, Ronson?'

'Don't you, mister?' fired back the sheriff. 'They're off of the Judge's fancy watch-chain, that's where. You seen him at the trial, lawyer. Always wears that fancy chain he does, but not yesterday.'

He gave a disgusted nod. 'Didn't come as no shock to me, I tell you. Maybe deep down I knew all along it was him that done it.'

Dropping the links back to the desk, Whiting gave a sceptical frown. 'That so? Still, looks like you've come up with the kind of evidence to nail him. Quite something, hey, Henry? Having the real killer sitting in the judge's chair. Blackitt must have some nerve!'

Henry found his voice at last. 'But why would Blackitt kill Juliet?'

Grover Whiting leaned back. 'He's got a temper, Henry. Could be he came back that night after you'd been there, and she told him she'd been talking to you.' He turned his gaze to Ronson again. 'So, you've got the evidence, sheriff. You going to do anything about it?'

Ronson scratched his chin. 'Having evidence is one thing. Making it stick, that's another.'

The lawyer laughed. 'So you're going to do nothing?'

'I didn't say that!' Ronson was a pathetic figure,

but as he spoke maybe in his eyes there was just a glimmer of the man he had been once, before he'd lost his family, and the drink had claimed his soul. 'I ain't never been much of a lawman. Done what I was told. I don't figure I got much time left in this trade. But maybe just once I can get something right. Do something good that my missus would of been proud of. I'm set on taking the judge down to the lock-up. Where he belongs.'

He shrugged despondently, 'Mind, arresting him's one thing. Keeping him locked up, well that's another. He owns most of this town, and most of the fellers in it one ways or another. Buy his way outa the grave he could. I'm gonna try, though. But I'm gonna need help.'

Henry eyed him carefully. 'What kind of help?'

'You're wearing a gun, mister,' said Ronson cautiously. 'And I know you can use it, I heard how you stood down Dan Finnegan on Main Street. City slicker maybe, but you're tough as nails.'

He heaved in a lungful of air. 'Blackitt's over at the Paradise. Not many customers in there right now. Two of us could take him.'

Mathilda grabbed at Henry's arm. 'You don't owe this man, or this town, anything, Henry.'

'I owe Luther Blackitt something,' he reminded her, as he shook her off. 'My brother'd still be alive if it wasn't for him. Hell, he was set on getting me kicking air for something he did. And once we get him behind bars then maybe we can start to get a few answers about Willis and his gang.'

She stepped back. 'If you can stay alive.'

Whiting stood up. 'I'd be glad to come along, too.'

Teale Ronson stared at him. 'Begging your

pardon, Mr Whiting, but when was the last time you toted a gun? I guess me and Deacon here can take him. Like I say, that's just a start. But I don't figure I got no choice.'

'Same goes for me,' said Henry. 'I'll mosey over to the Paradise with you, Ronson.'

'Henry! No ...'

But he was already following the lawman out of the door. It was still early, Charity hadn't rubbed the sleep out of its eyes yet, and few of Blackitt's cronies would be around. If the judge was going to get taken, then now was as good a time as any, he reckoned.

Ronson looked at him with a grudging respect as they started to cross the dusty street, then held back as a brace of wagons passed. 'I guess I'll owe you a real big favour after this, Deacon.'

'That's if either of us is still standing,' grunted Henry. 'Blackitt's like a snake. Could wriggle his way through a knothole.'

'Sure would have to be a big knothole,' commented the lawman, and they carried on over the street, onto the boardwalk and started moving down towards the ornate frontage of the saloon.

A young fellow in a greasy apron lounged in the doorway of a general store drinking a cup of coffee. 'Howdy sheriff,' he said amiably. 'How's business?'

'You just mind your own!' growled Ronson as they passed by.

The storeman laughed. 'Any time your pal feels like coming by to tell me and my customers about his night of forbidden passion, he's mighty welcome!'

Henry stopped, about to turn, and then thought

better of it, and caught up with the sheriff. Ronson glanced at him speculatively. 'It really happen that way did it?'

'What's that?'

'You and the gal. All night? I mean, you never said nothing to me.'

'You got the real killer now, Ronson,' Henry snapped testily. 'Maybe Mathilda and Mrs Peacock embroidered the facts some, maybe they didn't. Anyhow let's concentrate on hauling him in. You sure he's in the saloon?'

The sheriff nodded. 'Seen him as I come by on the way to Lawyer Whiting's place. Chewing the fat with the barkeep. Likely been there all night, with one of the girls.'

Henry remembered what Juliet had told him about Blackitt's nocturnal habits. 'Looking for someone to take Juliet's place?'

'Beats me what women see in him,' returned Ronson.

'They see money, and power,' said Henry. 'That's what.'

'Well, maybe we're going to put a stop to that.' Ronson came to a halt. A few more paces and they'd be at the saloon entrance. He hoisted out his heavy calibre sidearm, and Henry did likewise.

'We go straight in, Deacon, and if he pulls a gun, we shoot.'

'To kill?'

'Won't be no loss,' muttered the lawman sourly, and Henry saw that he was fast working out that a dead judge in the funeral parlour would be a whole lot less trouble to the town sheriff than a live one in the lock-up.

He clamped a warning hand on Ronson's wrist.

'You listen good, Ronson. Sure, if we have to we'll blow his wicked head off. But only if we have to. He's more trouble alive, sure, but maybe a lot more use. Locked up maybe he'll start to squawk to save his skin. There's a mighty big bunch of questions he could answer.'

Teale Ronson shrugged. 'Guess you might be right.' He shook himself nervously. 'You ready?'

'Whenever you say the word.'

The other man squared his sagging shoulders. 'Now's as good a time as any. Let's go!'

Stepping sharply forward, they turned through the door, and went in full tilt. Henry hadn't bargained on it being so shadowy in here after the bright morning sunlight. He squinted, getting his eyes to focus, and then saw Blackitt's bulk astride a stool at the curving bar counter. He had his back to them as he talked to the scrawny barkeep.

There was a noisy clatter of chairs and tables, as the sprinkling of other early customers made a dive for cover, knowing that if lead started flying about the place it wouldn't be too particular who it homed in on. The old Mexican Henry had seen the other morning, flung down his long-handled sweeping brush, and scuttled hastily into a dark corner.

'Luther Blackitt, you're under arrest!' Ronson's voice was hoarse, but surprisingly determined as he advanced towards the bar. The barkeep had vanished, speedily ducking down, and Blackitt ponderously shifted himself round, letting out a laugh of bellowing mockery.

'You just put that gun away, Teale Ronson, before you shoot yourself in the foot!'

'I'm giving the orders today! You hoist yourself

off of that stool, and get your hands up, judge.' Ronson edged nearer, and Henry stepped over the Mexican's discarded broom, moving pace by pace with the lawman, until they were just two or three yards from where the judge sat.

Blackitt made no attempt to move from where he was perched like a giant, beady-eyed vulture. He fixed on Henry with malevolent amusement. 'Thought you and that prissy little whore'd be out of Charity by now, Deacon.'

'You mind what you say about Mathilda!' snapped Henry. 'But if you're trying to rile me, you're wasting your time. Just do what the sheriff says. There's a cell waiting for you in the lock-up!'

Slowly, Blackitt eased himself down now, and reached round to where his hat lay on the polished counter.

'You take it slow now!' Ronson ordered twitchily.

Grinning contemptuously, Blackitt raised the hat slowly off the counter. 'See! No gun hidden under there.' He clamped the hat on his huge head. 'Now, you going to tell me what this charade's all about, Ronson?'

'You killed the woman, judge,' said the lawman. 'We got proof. And you'll hang for it.'

'Need a good strong rope to hang me, I'd say,' returned Blackitt lazily. 'Though it ain't ever going to get that far. It'll be you two buzzards swinging in the breeze.' He tugged at the brim of his hat. 'Hanging offence in Charity, accusing a judge of murder.'

He paused, and now he wasn't looking at either of them. 'Ain't that right, Hiram?'

Henry felt the hairs on the back of his neck bristle, and his nose wrinkled. All of a sudden there was something rancid in the air. He twisted round sharply.

'Just drop it, boy!' There was no mistaking that grating voice. The wizened figure stood framed in the doorway, flanked by two taller figures. Gliss pointed the sawn-off, heavy-bore shotgun straight at Henry's midriff. 'One move, and you'll be fighting to stuff your innards back inside of you!'

Henry let the weapon fall, and at the same time he heard Ronson's gun clatter to the floor. Now he was staring at Gliss's companions. Dan Finnegan to the left, that wasted face set in a sneer of hatred, and clad from head to toe in black, Wes Willis, leader of the Arizona Devils, stood to his right.

'You got some fine fellers working for you, Gliss,' he heard himself snarl. 'Though why they should take orders from a dried up old buzzard like you, beats me!'

In a rasping whisper, Teale Ronson said, 'Just keep your thoughts to yourself, Deacon.'

Dan Finnegan raised his heavy Navy Colt, and there was a loud, blood-freezing click as the hammer was thumbed back. 'You want me to finish them, Mr Gliss? It's be a real pleasure. 'Specially Deacon.'

Blackitt pushed past Henry, and said jovially. 'Nice to see you fellers again. You chose a good time to come calling.' He laughed, 'Saved me a couple of hours in the town lock-up. But maybe if you're going to finish these two, it'd be better to take 'em somewhere else.'

Gliss took a few steps forward, the shotgun swinging idly by his side. 'Sure,' he agreed, 'Deacon can wait.' Now, suddenly, he spat viciously, and swung the gun up again. 'But not you, judge. Your time has come!'

Blackitt stood there uncertainly, and watching him from behind, Henry could have sworn he saw his whole flabby body quiver. 'What's that you say?'

'Killed yourself a woman, I hear. That's a real waste. Juliet done you no harm.'

The judge gabbled, 'Hiram, listen up. She'd been talking to Deacon. And I didn't mean to kill her. Hell, you got a strange regard for female life all of a sudden. How about those gals back in Benson ...?'

'You talk too much, Blackitt. You ain't worth keeping alive ...'

Blackitt took a shivering step or two towards the stunted figure. 'Listen here, Gliss. Since when did you start taking decisions? You take orders same as I do. I want to talk to ...'

'Just following orders, judge!'

Even as Gliss spoke, both barrels roared, and the blast ripped viciously into Blackitt. Henry threw himself sideways to avoid the figure cannoning past him. The judge's torso was a mass of bloody shreds as he thundered against the bar, and then shot forward again, miraculously staying on his feet, the floor suddenly slippery with his blood. Swaying, he reached out a hand and then he toppled forward, and the whole floor shuddered as he hit the ground face down.

Momentarily dazed by the blast, Henry supported himself against the bar. Then, out of the corner of his eye he saw Teale Ronson move. It was probably the most foolhardy act the lawman had done in a long time, but there was some kind of doomed courage in it, too. Maybe, Henry found himself thinking in that split second, Ronson knew it was over for him but was determined to go down fighting. He was on his knees, his hand slicing towards the gun he'd dropped close to his feet.

His stubby fingers had just reached it when Dan Finnegan's slug caught him high on the chest, and he gave a low groan. Still on his knees he started to reach for the bloodied rent in his vest, then gave up the attempt, and looked round and up and his fading eyes found Henry. Ignoring Hiram Gliss's warning yell, Henry crouched down beside him. 'That's it then, Deacon ...' Ronson coughed. 'You're on your own now.'

Footsteps were coming smartly towards them, and Dan Finnegan stood there, an arrogant grin on his bony face. 'You need another slug to finish you, sheriff, I'd be glad to oblige.'

He raised his heavy pistol, but before he could fire again, Ronson slumped forward, and rolled onto his side. Henry stayed where he was, keeping his head down, expecting to hear another shot before a final blackness overwhelmed him.

Instead he heard Hiram Gliss's reedy voice. 'On your feet, Deacon. You got a touch longer in this world yet.'

'Do like Mr Gliss says, and quick!' snarled Finnegan, and aimed a kick at Henry, who ducked, and grabbed the gunman's ankle, giving an almighty heave.

Finnegan gave a yelp of surprise, and as he stumbled away, he tripped over the lifeless form of Judge Blackitt and went down on his back, arms flailing. Scrambling over the obscenely sticky floor, Henry found the nearest weapon. In one movement he grabbed the sweeping brush dropped by the old Mexican, and came to his feet, heaving the bristly head of the broom as hard as he could down into Finnegan's pale face.

Somewhere over to his left, he heard Hiram Gliss gave a screeching laugh. 'You take him if you can, Finnegan!'

Finnegan rolled away, and Henry's second blow missed him, but the movement took him further from where he'd dropped his revolver. With a boiling, mindless anger, Henry pursued Finnegan with the brush, swinging it round now, and using the handle as a kind of lance, jabbed out ferociously.

Finnegan blasted out a string of curses, and was halfway to his feet, when the end of the handle connected with his Adam's Apple. Giving a strangled squeal, he grabbed at his neck, choking for breath. His face was a mass of reddening scratches from his first encounter with the brush-head, and now he'd lost most of what little dignity he'd ever had.

Glancing round, Henry saw Gliss doubled up in malicious laughter. Wes Willis was watching too, but his face was impassive, and he showed no sign of coming to the aid of his henchman. Dropping the broom, Henry went for Finnegan again, this time with his fist. His knuckles met the other man's jaw with a painful but satisfying solid crunch, and Finnegan reeled back, lifting his arms to guard his face.

'If I'm going, I'm going down fighting!' yelled Henry, and closed with Finnegan, driving two quick stabs into the stomach. All the other man wanted now was to get away; he shuffled sideways, ducking one blow, and then Henry twisted round to get a better shot. He lifted Finnegan's head with a sharp uppercut, and followed it with a sledgehammer blow which sent Finnegan skidding back, towards the door. He came to a halt as he crashed into Hiram Gliss, who was still cackling with a devilish merriment.

'Git off of me!' he protested, the amusement vanishing, and he shoved Finnegan away with a bony hand. The dazed man stumbled into Wes Willis, who gripped his collar, keeping him upright.

'Right, you've had your fun, Gliss. We got better things to do than watch this one being chased round a saloon.'

For a second or two, nobody was looking at Henry. He snatched the slim chance he was being offered. Grabbing up a revolver as he went, he skated, rather than ran towards where Gliss stood glowering at the semi-conscious Finnegan. At the last instant Gliss spotted him coming, but it was too late. Henry shouldered into him, propelling him sideways, and got his arm round the scrawny neck. He yanked Gliss back, and jammed the muzzle against a misshapen ear.

A surge of triumph went through him. It seemed like against all the odds, he might just get out of this. Except that Wes Willis, thrusting Finnegan away from him, was looking awful casual and unconcerned.

'You go ahead and fire, Deacon,' he said laconically. 'Hiram ain't going to be too much of a loss to anyone.'

'Now lookee here ...' Gliss began to struggle, but thought better of it as Henry threatened to push the gun right through his eardrum.

Willis hooked his thumbs in his gunbelt. 'Bring them in, boys.'

Henry's hope faded at once as Mathilda and Grover Whiting were pushed roughly into the saloon. Willis reached out and grabbed her by the hair. She screamed, and he laughed, as another of his men came up alongside them and pressed a gun roughly against the girl's cheek.

Willis yawned. 'By the time we finished, Deacon, this here whole floor's gonna be painted red. I'd say that by pulling that trigger you'll cause yourself a lot more pain than you'll cause me. Gliss dies, and this lady'll be missing most of her brains.'

'They'll kill us all anyway, Henry!' shouted Mathilda defiantly, and winced as Willis dragged at her hair again.

'Maybe,' Henry muttered, as he did the only thing he could do, and released his hold on Gliss. The weapon was snatched from him, and he smiled wanly at Mathilda. 'We're not dead yet.'

He reeled as Gliss brought the muzzle of the revolver against the side of his jaw with a teeth-rattling blow. 'Not yet, maybe. But you ain't got long left, Deacon!'

TEN

'How're you doing, Mr Whiting?'

The elderly lawyer was hunched up towards the front end, wedging himself back against the side of the wagon and making an effort to keep his balance against the interminable rocking and jolting. That wasn't too easy with your hands tied tight behind your back, and all three captives were bruised and aching from being hurled around as Gliss and his men headed back through the rough terrain on the edge of the mountains.

Even so, Grover Whiting managed a fair impression of a smile. 'I've been more comfortable, Henry, but I guess I'm surviving.'

Up front, without turning round, the wagon driver barked, 'You keep your noise down in there. Save your voices for when we get to Diamond Rock!' He cackled coarsely.

'You tell it to 'em, Chuck!' yelled someone, and his laugh was taken up by the others, rippling through the riders flanking the second of the two wagons.

Henry looked at Mathilda. She had a swelling bruise on her cheek from where that bastard had jabbed her with the gun back at the Paradise. His jaw was still aching intolerably from where Gliss had lammed into him with the pistol, and all things considered, the three of them made a pitiful exhibition here in the half-light of their swaying prison.

He was real sorry that the lawyer had been dragged into this, though. He wasn't a young man, and he'd been unfortunate enough to be in the wrong place at the wrong time, when some of Willis's men had burst into his office. They'd clearly come after Mathilda, and if he hadn't put up a struggle, maybe they would have left him there. He'd taken a bloodied nose in the scuffle, but truth to tell, thought Henry, he was mighty lucky they hadn't killed him. There was no accounting for Hiram Gliss's whims, though.

'Bring him along, for the ride as well.' That corrupted face had twisted into a leer. 'He's a legal man. He can do my marrying, back up in Diamond Rock!'

It said a lot for Charity's sense of public duty and neighbourliness that the streets had miraculously emptied while all this was going on. Not that he could blame them. They'd know well enough who the riders on the big horses were, and, human nature being what it was, self-preservation generally won out over any higher feelings. Now they'd likely be congratulating themselves that their own town had got off pretty lightly compared to so many others after a visit from the Arizona Devils. Blackitt was dead, sure, and Teale Ronson, but neither of them were going to leave a big hole in anyone's heart.

Mathilda shuffled closer to him. 'We're in a bad way, Henry, aren't we?'

'In a touch of trouble, sure.' He managed to edge

nearer her, and she pressed her head onto his shoulder. 'But as Chet Stookey would say, we're not dead till they nail down the lid.' He grinned ruefully, 'But doesn't seem he's going to get that frilly garter I promised him.'

'Garter?' For a moment, maybe, she forgot what they were, and looked at him suspiciously. 'Where from?'

'From the leg of one of the Paradise girls,' he told her. 'Old Chet's dream.'

'And what's your dream?' Mathilda asked, 'Something more decent than that, I hope?'

He caught a whiff of her perfume. 'I don't reckon I'd better tell you that …'

He knew she was smiling, and then someone twitched aside the canvas flap at the back of the wagon, and Dan Finnegan's battered face looked in, with a lewdly twisted grin. 'There's a pretty picture, now. Ain't much you two folk can do to each other with your hands tied, is there? And I don't reckon Mr Gliss'll want his bride nosing up to another man so close to the wedding! Maybe I should ride up to the lead wagon, and tell him what's going on. If you're real nice to him, maybe he'll let you ride up front with him.'

'I'm staying here. With my friends!' Mathilda flared out. 'And who says I'm marrying Gliss?'

Finnegan sneered. 'He does. You got no say in the matter, missie. And being as how you're kinda … damaged goods, you oughta think yourself lucky.' The sneer turned into a grin as the wagon heaved itself over another rocky patch and Mathilda was unable to stop herself sliding away from Henry towards the lawyer.

Now Finnegan's eyes burned into Henry. 'And

you got a real party waiting for you, mister. We know how to enjoy ourselves in Diamond Rock!'

He dropped the flap back, and they heard him laughing as he rode off. Mathilda's eyes were big with fear, but now she said nothing. Right now, it seemed that all Gliss wanted was to take possession of something he thought was his. If he had any inkling of the secret they all shared, then he'd shown no sign of it. Things were unpleasant enough, but they might get a whole lot more tricky if he found out who Mathilda really was.

Henry flexed his shoulders again. Most of the feeling had gone from his hands. Finnegan had insisted on tying him, and the rope had carved canyon-deep-weals into his flesh. Now his fingers were numb, and there was no way in heaven he was going to do anything clever like saw through his bonds by rubbing them against the piece of sharply broken board close to his head.

He twisted to look out through the gap provided by the splintered planking. Wasn't much of a view, though a while back he'd caught sight of Marty Wilson's place. It wasn't much comfort to him to recall their escape from that particular prison. Lightning might strike the same place more than once, but you couldn't bargain on the US cavalry being so predictable.

There wasn't a whole lot to see now. They were starting to climb through the outhills of the Chiricahuas, up a narrow defile bounded by rising, knife-edged rocks, aiming inexorably for Hiram Gliss's own stony slab of empire. His thoughts started to wander round the unpleasant subject of Gliss, and he tried to recall what Luther Blackitt had said, just before the shotgun blast had torn him apart.

Eventually it echoed back at him: '*You take orders same as I do*.' Henry nodded. That made sense. Wes Willis and his thugs weren't the sort to dance to any tune played by a runt-backed specimen like Gliss. Of course, it could be that Willis was running things; but then Blackitt would surely have appealed to him to spare his worthless life. Well, it didn't much matter now either way who was pulling the strings on this evil outfit.

Turning his head again, he peered out through his narrow window on the passing world, straining his eyes painfully to look up and maybe see the sky. He didn't see the sky, just the topmost point of a jagged-edge rock. Then as he was about to turn back again, he spotted a shadowy movement up there.

Before he could let out a shout, outside all hell was let loose, as a blistering volley of gunfire poured down from the surrounding rocks onto the little convoy. Several slugs ripped through the canvas wagon-top and pressing himself down, he shimmied over to Mathilda. 'Lie flat!' he yelled, 'And you, Mr Whiting!'

'What in blind Hades is going on out there?' shouted the lawyer, awkwardly tipping himself forward onto his belly.

Their wagon was still moving forward, but now they heard someone bellow, 'Cut the frigging traces, Chuck, and get yourself under cover!'

A moment later and the wagon came to a halt as the frightened team-horses were set free. The fellow who'd been driving was under the wagon now, blasting off wildly with a repeating rifle. The noise was deafening. All round they could hear the outlaws sending back their own leaden rain into the rocks. Horses whinnied and screamed, and now above them the canvas flapped wildly as more bullets sliced into it.

'It's Apaches!' Henry gasped. 'I just saw one of them up on a ridge. Hell, there must be a whole army of them up there!'

Mathilda swallowed a scream. 'Oh my God, Henry. I don't want them to get me. I've heard stories ...'

He wished he could put his arms round her, to protect her in some way, but he was helpless. They were trapped. Escaping from Gliss into the hands of Apache renegades was no escape at all.

He got the feeling that the gunfire was slackening off. There was no sound from underneath the wagon now, and the driver had plainly been hit. Suddenly the canvas flap was ripped aside. It was Dan Finnegan again, and this time he was clambering in. Henry had never seen a man so frightened; there was total terror contorting that scratched and dirtied face.

'Help me!' he shouted.

Henry stared in disbelief. 'Help you? How in hell can we ...?'

Then, another figure hoisted itself over the backboard. The Indian was nearly naked, with a filthy bandanna round his head, jet black hair scraping his shoulders. A muscular hand shot out, and he hauled Finnegan back by his shirt, and all but threw him back outside, and dived in pursuit.

'No, please, wait, I'll ...' Dan Finnegan's words died in a bubbling scream. Moments later, the backboard was let down, and three staring Apaches stood there, with a queer kind of puzzlement on their swarthy faces.

They noticed Mathilda swiftly enough, even though she desperately tried to squirm behind Henry. One of them pointed and said something quick and guttural to his companions, which raised a raucous laugh from all three of them. Then another Apache appeared behind them, taller, older maybe. He studied them, narrow-eyed and impassive, and then barked something at the three braves in front of him. They were plainly reluctant to move, but with a final menacingly interested look at the girl, they disappeared from view.

The tall Indian stood there a moment longer, and then he was gone too. For now, they were to be left alone, it seemed. There were a few more sporadic gunshots, but it was clear that the battle, such as it had been, was over.

In the wagon, the three prisoners huddled together, not speaking. They stayed there like that for maybe thirty minutes, saw nobody, but heard plenty. Now and then there was an agonised scream, and it was chillingly plain that the outlaws who hadn't died in the initial ambush were wishing that they had. Grover Whiting sat there, sheet-white and silent, while Mathilda was humming loudly to herself, her eyes shut tight, trying to hide the noise of what was happening out there beyond their wooden walls.

Henry couldn't help but listen, in a kind of numbed, horrified fascination. Then they started on Hiram Gliss, and he wished that some kindly providence would send him deaf. Gliss deserved a lot of things, but not what they were doing to him. At first his shouting and pleading was almost coherent.

'I tell you, you painted savages, if this is all about

that whisky, I never knowed it was bad. I wouldn't sell no-one poisoned whisky ...'

Perhaps Gliss had hit on the truth, that this was no random attack. Juliet's story about his fraudulent dealings with the Indians hiding out in the mountains near Diamond Rock must be true. Gliss had tried to trade with the devil, and now the devil had come to claim his soul.

None of his tormentors took any heed of what Gliss was trying to say. In any case, soon after that, even Henry couldn't understand what he was saying. A sour bile rose in his throat, as just a few yards away Gliss gibbered and screeched, and shrieked in a wild, hopeless, litany. Then mercifully, at last, his noise too was stopped.

Drawing in a long breath, Henry looked at Mathilda, and found himself praying. The Indians had finished the first part of the business, now he heard them moving round outside, chatting away to each other, sometimes laughing, like they were just tidying up after a party. Once a brave came round and looked in at them, but after a second or two of interested staring he ducked down, and Henry realised with a shudder that Dan Finnegan's corpse was receiving a few final attentions.

Then, suddenly, it went quiet. There were horses shifting restlessly around out there: and they heard the jingle of a trace chain now and again, or the soft snicker of one of the animals. But no human sounds.

'I figure they've gone.' Henry realised it was a good hour since he'd spoken, and his voice sounded hollow in his head.

Alongside him, Mathilda jerked. She'd been hunched there in a state which was neither awake nor asleep. 'They're still there, Henry,' she said huskily. 'Just waiting for us to come out.'

'And why'd they do that?' he asked. 'They could have come in at any time. Seems to me that they were after revenge on Gliss. That tall feller was the chief, I reckon. He saw we were prisoners. Maybe he figured we deserved to be let alone.'

Grover Whiting nodded. 'You might be right, Henry. They've got a weird code of honour in their own way, I'm told.'

'But suppose they are still out there?' Mathilda burst out. 'Just waiting. Biding their time.' She stared out through the open end of the wagon, and then let out a shriek as someone moved into their view.

The man standing there, staring in at them had come round the side of the wagon as silent as a ghost. Too solid to be a phantom, though. He was broad-shouldered, his beard mostly grey, and his face burned to lined leather by a lifetime in the outdoors.

Mathilda let out a rolling sob of relief. 'Sam. Sam McWheel! What are you doing here?'

The old-timer scrambled in agilely, and it was a second's work for him to slice deftly through their bonds. Mathilda had collapsed in tears now, and he put fatherly arms round her. 'Hey, that's no kinda greeting for your old pal. Since you wouldn't come to me, I figured I'd best ride back to Charity and come look for you.'

He glanced sideways to where the two men were sitting, rubbing their wrists. Grimly, he said, 'Been quite a party out there. I was listening to the shooting a couple miles back.'

'They're all dead?'

'Sure. Dead as mutton and kinda ... butchered.'

Mathilda pulled back from him. 'It was terrible, Sam. Cooped up in here, and listening to ...'

'Better cooped up in here than being out there,' McWheel said phlegmatically, and rolled himself a smoke. 'But I figure you'll have to stay in here a while longer, Mathilda. Me and these fellers got things to do afore I let you come out.'

She swallowed hard. 'It's bad out there?'

'Worse'n I've seen in a long time,' he confirmed grimly. 'One thing's sure, the Arizona Devils've gone to hell in a big way!'

Mathilda nodded. 'I'd better introduce you, Sam. These gentlemen'll know who you are, I guess. They ... um ... they know all about me, too.'

He blinked speculatively, 'Do they now? And how'd that be?'

'It's a long story,' she said dully, 'This is Henry Deacon, from California. And Mr Whiting. He's a lawyer.'

Sam McWheel snapped a lucifer into flame, and lit his cigarette. He sucked on it thoughtfully. 'Well, I figure stories can wait. You both feel up to giving me a hand out there? We got us some digging to do. They're scum, no doubt. 'Specially Gliss. But we ain't leaving them to the buzzards and the wolves.'

Even when he was an old man, Henry would sometimes wake in the night, wringing with sweat as the nightmare of that scene outside returned to his sleeping mind. Death had its own smell, sure, but its own sound, too; the buzz of flies already clouding the air above each hacked body, and maybe it was that busy, commonplace sound which made the whole gut-wrenching business worse.

Luckily there wasn't much digging to be done. Just off the trail they found a wide, deep fissure where a rock had been split by some long ago shifting of the earth. Between them they carried and dragged the remains of the men who had terrorised Arizona and heaved them into it.

Some instinct made them leave Hiram Gliss till last. He lay on his back close to the wagon; his eyes open staring at the sky where buzzards circled hopefully. Henry retched and looked away. 'Why'd they do that to all of them, McWheel? It's inhuman...'

'Well, I guess they figure that being only half a man for the rest of eternity's a pretty fair punishment ...' In one movement he hoisted the stripped, mutilated body over his shoulder, and strode over to the makeshift tomb.

He came back, and rolled another smoke for himself, offering the makings to Henry, who fashioned a cigarette with shaking fingers. Whiting was slumped back against one of the wagon wheels, clearly drained by the effort. McWheel called to Mathilda. 'I guess you can come out now.'

As he helped her down, she looked warily round her. There were plenty of signs of what had happened here. Three dead horses; pieces of clothing here and there; telltale dark stains on the stony ground. She took a deep breath. 'It looks like the Apaches have done our job for us then, Sam.' She glanced to where the lawyer leaned against the wheel, 'And there was no need for you to send that wire after all, Mr Whiting.'

The grizzled old timer flicked away a spent lucifer, and blinked curiously. 'What wire'd that be, Mr Whiting?'

'You mustn't blame Mathilda,' Henry cut in speedily, 'I figured she needed help. It was me told Mr Whiting to wire Washington.' He scowled, 'And this plan you and your ... Old Man ... cooked up was real crazy, as far as I can see.'

Sam grunted, 'Which maybe ain't so far. We needed to catch these boys out in the open. Needed some notion of where they were planning to go next. Someone close to Gliss could of found out that kind of thing ...'

'Would you want to get close to Gliss?' demanded Henry.

Mathilda moved by his side. 'It's done now, Sam, anyhow.' Henry put his arm round her. 'I guess I'm finished as a US marshal. But at least the Arizona Devils are finished too. I'm safe. You're safe ...'

'Shouldn't be so sure of that, girlie!'

Henry jerked round, and his blood froze at the sight of Wes Willis standing on a flat topped rock seven or eight yards from them. There was something almost demonic about the sight of him, black as the devil, with the Winchester aimed unwavering at them.

Mathilda sagged, and Henry supported her, keeping his arm round her. 'The Indians didn't get you, then?' he said hoarsely.

'Maybe they did,' returned Willis. 'And I've come back.'

'You ain't no spirit,' grunted Sam McWheel. 'Riding up ahead was you, when the Apaches hit? And jus' kept riding.'

Willis laughed. 'A man'd be a fool to die 'less he had to. You unhorse that gun of yours, Sam McWheel. I guess that's who you are. I've spotted you a couple times up in Diamond Rock. Didn't quite figure you for a miner.'

McWheel hoisted out his six-gun and let it fall. 'How come you know my name, Willis?'

'I told him.' Grover Whiting moved round in front of them, and stooping, picked up Sam's gun. He was weary no longer. Stepping back, he surveyed the three of them with a wry, mocking smile. Without looking at Willis, up on the rock behind him, he said, 'Hard to tell who was who out of what was left of the boys, Willis. But I didn't figure any of those remains to be yours.'

'You, Whiting? You're behind all this?'

'I'm proud to say I am,' returned the lawyer in response to Henry's hoarse question. 'I've kept Washington on the hop for a good year now.'

Triumph was etched into his laugh, and Henry suddenly saw what he hadn't seen before about Grover Whiting. There was a gnawing vanity in a man like this, with his twitchy little beard which would need careful clipping every morning; in his manicured nails. Vain men never admitted their own faults, but blamed everyone else, and that made them as dangerous as a buffalo with toothache. Whiting's next words confirmed it. 'I got treated like dirt up there. Nobody wanted to know a back-country lawyer like me. Well, I given them a good run, I'd say.'

'And never mind who gets hurt? How about that little girl up in Papillon?' asked Henry, bitterly.

Whiting shrugged. 'You fret about other folk, Henry, you get nowhere. Now me'n Wes here've got a sizeable pouch of cash to split now that everyone else has … resigned!'

Sam McWheel scratched his nose. 'So you never

sent no wire to Washington, then?'

'That wouldn't have been too clever, would it?' Whiting was amused at that. 'But I figured there'd be no harm in making out that I was a prisoner along with these two. Nobody knew what you looked like, see, except Mathilda here. Thought she'd be able to point you out to me when we got to Diamond Rock.'

Mathilda broke away from Henry. 'So that struggle in your office was just play-acting?'

He raised the gun warningly. 'You're a fine one to talk about play-acting, young lady. Now you just move back a step or two.'

'You made sure my brother got killed, didn't you?' Henry stormed. Rage billowed through him. 'Hell, Whiting, those Apaches are like Sunday preachers compared to you.'

'A lawman down near the Mex border got Stretch Finnegan in the back with a lucky shot. When your brother came nosing round, I reckoned Stretch could earn his keep a while longer by acting as a murder victim.' Whiting shook his head, and went on mildly. 'Anyhow, I sent your brother back to you, didn't I? I figured that seeing what had happened to him would ... well, quieten his kinfolk. Hadn't bargained on you coming all the way from California. Still, don't make no difference now. We'll fix you up so's it looks like the Apaches got you, too. Hey Wes?'

Willis had just been standing there impassively while all this was going on. He grinned. 'I'm all for fixing things up, Mr Whiting. Fixing them up real neat. For me, though. Nobody else. I took all the risks, riding up front of the devil riders, so I figure I take all the money.'

A look of alarm began to spread over the lawyer's thin face, and he started to swing round. The brittle explosion of a single rifle shot echoed and re-echoed off the surrounding rocks, and Whiting, his shirt front suddenly dripping crimson staggered forward a couple of paces. He was just starting to raise the revolver, when a second shot lanced through the swirling dust, taking him in the side of the head, and he catapulted sideways with a despairing, dying moan.

As he fell, Sam's revolver tumbled out of his hand, and slid away over the stony ground, stopping at Mathilda's feet. Some moments had a way of seeming to stretch out into a lifetime. Henry began to open his mouth as he saw Mathilda drop to her knees and snatch at the pistol. He started to move towards her, still on the edge of forming any words. She whipped up the revolver, holding it two-handed, aiming it at the man on the rock. Two shots blasted out so close you couldn't have slipped a frog-hair between them, and Mathilda toppled forward onto her face, right next to where Grover Whiting lay. One half of his face was a mishapen mask of blood and splintered bone. His eyes were still open, staring blindly at the woman slumped beside him.

The one they called the Old Man settled himself in the narrow armchair, and ran a hand through his white hair. He looked at Sam McWheel who was in the middle of raising a cup of coffee to his lips. 'I've racked my brains, Sam, trying to think if I ever come across Grover Whiting in Washington. If I did ever meet him, I've long forgotten.'

'I guess that's one of the things that most riled

him.'

Mathilda sat on the sagging sofa with Henry by her side. Willis's last shot had grazed her shoulder. Her bullet had caught him smack between the eyes. A lucky shot, maybe, but then Henry reckoned they'd been in line for some of that.

The Old Man reflected on what she'd just said. 'Wasted his life, fretting about what he might have been. Could have made something of himself out here …' He looked round as Mrs Peacock came in, bringing him a cup of coffee.

She was determined not to be overawed by this important visitor who'd come all the way from Washington with a personal message of thanks from the President himself. 'You're lucky I don't tip this in your lap, mister,' she said shortly. 'You and your crazy ideas. This girl could of got herself killed or worse.'

He blinked, 'What's worse than getting killed, ma'am?'

'Marrying Hiram Gliss for one!' she snapped back.

Mathilda leaned forward. 'Let's just get one thing straight, shall we? Nobody forced me to take part in all this. Maybe Sam did cook up the idea, but I threw in a few of the ingredients myself!' She half turned to look at Henry. 'Hadn't bargained on this one coming along to stir the pot, too, though.'

The Old Man sipped his coffee thoughtfully. 'Seems to me I might be able to use you again, Mathilda. There's things a woman can do that a man can't.'

Mathilda giggled. 'I guess there are, sir.'

He scowled with a mixture of embarrassment and amusement. 'Maybe I could've put that better.

Thing is we got us some trouble down in New Mexico. And I'd say the person behind it all is a certain hard-faced lady who runs herself a saloon. Maybe you could get yourself a job there and …'

Henry sprang to his feet. 'Hold it right there, mister. I'm not having Mathilda going off to New Mexico.'

'Aren't you now?' said Mathilda sharply. 'And who asked you for your opinion?'

Sam McWheel shifted in his chair and gave a sorrowful shake of his head. 'You ain't asked her to marry you yet, have you, Henry? Hell, I always knowed California folk was lazy'n slow. Takes 'em all day to make up their minds to get outa bed.'

'Don't you talk about Henry like that!' exclaimed Mathilda, turning on him. She shrugged, 'Though it's true, he hasn't made me any offers yet. And I'm not sure I like the idea of being some sweet little home-maker back in California, cooking a man's meals, washing diapers …'

Henry clapped his hands. 'Do I get to finish what I was saying?' He paused, and as silence fell, he went on. 'I'm not figuring on going back to California. Not to stay, anyhow. And there'd be worse places to settle down than Charity. Now we've got Marty Wilson as sheriff things'll start to get cleaned up, quieted down. I've sold the business in 'Frisco. I kind of like the idea of starting up again somewhere new, somewhere growing.'

The Old Man chuckled, 'Ain't much call for a shipping business here in Charity, is there?'

'Maybe not,' agreed Henry. 'But one business it's much the same as another. And what Charity needs is a real fine livery. I got the money to set one up, but what I don't know about horses'd fill a good-sized library.'

He glanced down at Mathilda. 'So I'm on the lookout for a someone who can fill that gap in my education.'

Mathilda blinked, 'You just want me as a business partner, Henry?'

Mrs Peacock laughed, 'Nothing to stop you washing a few diapers on the side, Mathilda. Ain't that right, Henry?'

He folded his arms. 'If you folk don't mind, I'd rather get on with … negotiating with this good lady in private.' He spoke to Mathilda again. 'Care to take a stroll in the sunshine, ma'am, to discuss this further?'

'I guess so,' She got to her feet with a promising grin. 'A stroll in the sunshine sounds like a real good idea.'